EMERALDS

OTHER TITLES BY K.A. LINDE

EMERALDS

k.a. linde

Emeralds, All That Glitters, Book 2.5

By K.A. Linde

Copyright © 2015 by K.A. Linde

All rights reserved.

Cover Designer: Sarah Hansen, Okay Creations, www.okaycreations.com

Editor and Interior Designer: Jovana Shirley, Unforeseen Editing, www.unforeseenediting.com

Visit my website at www.kalinde.com

ISBN-13: 978-1518771859

To Jessica,
Without you, this book would have never existed.

ONE

Summer Before College

FREEDOM WAS THE SOUND OF THE SUBWAY whisking through the tunnels and screeching to a halt at Trihnity Hamilton's stop in Greenwich Village. It was walking off the train and emerging onto the busy streets of Manhattan above. It was knowing that, in three months' time, *this* would be her life.

Trihn sighed happily and maneuvered the busy streets with practiced ease. Her sister, Lydia's, apartment was right around the block, and Trihn would be moving in at the end of the summer to attend fashion design school. She was already visualizing where all the new things she had purchased would go when she moved out of her parent's townhouse in Brooklyn.

With her head in the clouds, she traipsed up the stone stairs to Lydia's building. As she was punching in the code to enter, the door violently swung open. Trihn yelped as it crashed toward her. She jumped backward, just barely missing getting hit in the face.

"Jesus Christ!" she yelled.

The door hit the wall and ricocheted back toward the person who had thrown it open in such haste.

"Why don't you watch what you're doing?" she asked.

She picked up her dance bag where it had landed on the stairs two steps below the entrance. She hadn't even realized she had thrown it, and now, her shoulder was throbbing. *Great.*

"Oh, shit! I'm sorry," the guy said. He roughly grabbed the door in his hand and eased it back open.

She rolled her shoulder back and cringed. If she didn't have the use of her shoulder, she was going to be fucked at ballet later tonight. She could not have this two weeks before the Senior Showcase.

"Yeah, well"—Trihn shifted her dance bag to the other shoulder and winced—"be more careful next time."

"Sorry. I will. Are you all right?" he asked, taking a step toward her.

Her eyes drifted upward, and she forgot all about her hurt shoulder.

This guy was hot. She'd seen all manner of gorgeous men while modeling during the past two years, but this guy was different—less of a pretty boy with no coifed hair, oil-slicked body, or perfectly waxed…everything.

He wore a fit NYU T-shirt and running shorts that accentuated his muscular physique. He had sandy-blond hair that wasn't flawlessly groomed. Some of it fell into his electric-blue eyes when he looked at her. Concern was written on his face, and she felt her body humming to its own tune when he smiled at her.

"Um...yeah. My shoulder. Dance."

Am I even coherent?

He smiled wider. "Sorry about that. I didn't know anyone was on the other side."

She cleared her throat and shrugged her dance bag higher. *Why is his smile so disarming?*

"Don't worry about it."

"Seriously, are you sure your shoulder is all right?"

She dropped her bag and then dramatically rolled both shoulders to show him that she was fine. But then she flinched, ruining the effect. "Actually, I'm not sure. We'll see how it goes."

"Well, let me give you my number, and if you need to see a doctor or anything, you can give me a call."

Trihn ignored the flutter in her stomach. "Sure. I don't think I'll have to go but just in case."

Right. Just in case.

Trihn handed over her phone, and he punched in his name and number. Before she could take it back, he clicked the Send button.

He smiled at her again. "Now, I'll know it's you," he explained.

Yeah. Definite flutters.

She glanced down at the screen. "Preston."

"That's me. And you are?"

"Trihn. Um…Trihnity, though my friends call me Trihn."

"You know you have a church named after you," he joked.

She laughed. "Yeah, so I've heard. It's on the other side of Washington Square Park. And I'm pretty sure it's not named after me."

"You're probably right." He ran a hand back through his messy hair.

Then, they stood there for a minute in charged silence. He seemed like he wanted to say something else, but he held his tongue. She felt as if her black Louboutin heels should carry her across the short distance into the building, but she didn't move.

In fact, she didn't even want to move.

It had been a long time since she had met a guy whom she paid more than a second's notice. Between school, modeling, and the dance company, she'd had zero time for guys. Sure, she'd had plenty of flings— make-out sessions in Prague, dirty-dancing in London, flirtations across multiple borders—but nothing long term. Lydia always said she was too young to be so serious about her work. Though Lydia was the exact opposite, so Trihn hadn't even bothered to listen to that.

But now, Trihn had put modeling behind her. In two weeks, her time as a company member at the New York City Dance House would come to a close. There would just be school. Perhaps she should give in to the one guy who had turned her eye.

"Let me get that," Preston said. He reached down, snatched her bag up, and swung the door wide, holding it open for her. "Here. After you."

"Thanks." She bit her lip and pushed her long brown-to-blonde ombre hair off her shoulders.

This was her moment. This was where she should say something, be more like Lydia. *What would my wild child sister do?* Probably lean into her hip, touch his arm, hold him hypnotized in her captive gaze. She'd toss her hair and casually ask him to dinner without a second thought. It was her way.

Trihn was confident but not like Lydia who would go through boyfriends as frequently as her mood changed and never feared rejection.

Trihn opened her mouth to say something and then closed it.

No, she couldn't do it.

She wasn't Lydia. That much she was sure of.

If he wanted to pursue her, then he would. He had her phone number after all. She shouldn't expect more than that while meeting for the first time even if some intense energy was coursing between them.

"I appreciate it." She grabbed her bag out of his hand. "I didn't mean to keep you from wherever you were off to in a rush."

"Oh, right," he said as if he had just remembered that the only reason they were talking was because he had nearly slammed the door into her. "Well, I hope you feel better. Maybe I'll see you around."

Is that an invitation?

"Sure. I'd like that," she said with a winning smile.

His eyes met hers again, and she felt her stomach do a full-on somersault. Her smile widened, and she looked at him through hooded eyes and dark black lashes. If Preston didn't know she was interested at this point, then he was the most oblivious man on the planet.

He looked as if he were debating on saying something more. Instead, he finally took a step backward and nodded his head. "It was nice meeting you, Trihn. Let me know about that shoulder."

"Will do," she murmured.

As he jogged down the stairs and out of sight, she sighed heavily, losing the bounce in her step from earlier. *Damn, maybe I should have just asked him out.*

At least next year, there would be plenty of hot guys in the city to go out with. She had just graduated from high school last weekend and would be at NYU starting in September. No need to rush into anything.

She couldn't help the pang of disappointment anyway.

Oh, well.

Next year.

TWO

TRIHN TRUDGED UP THE STAIRS to Lydia's second-floor apartment. She knocked on the door and waited impatiently, still on edge about what had just transpired.

How come I could flirt with half a dozen guys in other countries when I was modeling but not have one reasonable conversation with a hot guy I can actually *date?*

It was so frustrating. This was why she didn't bother with this shit. Maybe the language barrier was better. Kissing had made so much more sense to her in other countries where the guys all spoke half-coherent broken English.

The door popped open, and Lydia's glowing face smiled back at her. "Trihn!" she cried. "There you are! I didn't know if you would still be coming over before dance!"

"Yeah, sorry. I got held up," Trihn said dismissively.

No point in telling her what had happened. Lydia never would have let Preston get away without a promise of a future meeting.

"Well, get your ass in here. I just had an epiphany about the living room for when you move in!" Lydia said.

Trihn laughed as she followed her sister. "When did you die your hair blonde?"

Lydia shrugged. "Two days ago?"

Of course.

Lydia would change her hair color with her mood, just like how she'd change the guy she was seeing.

Even though they were sisters, they couldn't be more different. Trihn and Lydia had acquired different marks from their parents' mixed ancestry—Vietnamese, Brazilian, and a melting pot of European roots. Trihn was tall, lean, and exotic with high cheekbones, green eyes that slanted upward at the corners just like her mother's, and her dark-as-night natural hair. Lydia looked more like their father. She was of medium height with dark brown eyes with gold rings and hair that she always parted down the middle. She was energetic, drew all manner of people to her like no one else Trihn had ever met, and had a proclivity for eccentricity.

Trihn usually just called her a hippie to get on her nerves, but today, with the new blonde look, long maroon skirt, and crocheted cream crop, she looked every inch the hippie. Trihn had always been more of a rocker, like how she looked now in the shortest high-waist cutoff jeans she owned, a studded sheer black top, and sky-high designer heels. Yet they were sisters, and for that reason alone, their differences never mattered.

"What epiphany did you have?" Trihn asked. She tossed her dance bag down on the couch and moved her shoulder. It was still hurting. She immediately started doing stretches to try to work out the pain.

"Okay, so I was thinking that once you move in, we could collage this entire wall," Lydia said, spreading her arms wide. "We could put up pictures from my photography classes and your fashion projects. Oh, modeling shots! We could even do a dance shoot. I'm sure I have my old pointe shoes around here somewhere."

Lydia disappeared into her room to look for her toe shoes from when she had been a part of the NYC Dance House as well. Trihn just shook her head and followed after her. She plopped down on Lydia's bed that basically touched the ground.

"Here they are!"

"Ly," Trihn said, "we have three months to figure out how we're going to decorate. Shouldn't we just wait until Tasha moves out? Then, I could move in what I have, and we could see what we actually need."

Lydia's shoulders dropped dramatically as she sighed. She tossed the shoes onto her cluttered desk. "Please, Trihn, try to have less enthusiasm about the fact that we're going to have the coolest apartment in all of Manhattan in a few months."

"I'm excited. It's just not happening yet. We both have other things to worry about until then."

"What do I have to worry about? I have the summer off!" Lydia proclaimed.

"Aren't you interning?"

Lydia brushed her hair over one shoulder and smiled forlornly. "Right, I'm interning at a fashion magazine in the photography department. It's just what I've always wanted to do…to follow in Mom and Dad's footsteps."

That was how their parents had met in the first place. Their mother had been the head of acquisitions for the fashion magazine where their father had sold his work to at the time. Their mom had pulled a lot of strings to get Lydia this opportunity. Of course, she was being blasé about it and would rather spend the summer working on her art.

"It's a great opportunity."

"Whatever. Tell me about you! Are you excited about the Senior Showcase?" Lydia asked. Her voice filled with longing. "I so wish I were still in the company."

"Well, I'll never outshine you. That's for sure. We both know that you were always better at ballet than I was."

"But you love it more," Lydia conceded.

Trihn smiled brightly. She had always loved dance in all forms. The company focused so much energy on ballet, but she was excited that her dance for Senior Showcase was going to be a contemporary piece from her favorite choreographer at the studio. She would leave it to her best friend, Renée, to perform the beautiful ballet solo.

"I just can't believe that it will all be over in two weeks," Trihn said.

"Then, you can spend the whole summer with me."

"Aren't you going to be swamped?"

Lydia was such a dreamer. Trihn swore that if Lydia didn't have to work, she would spend the rest of her life daydreaming, writing poetry, growing a garden, and drinking.

"Oh, right. Work." She stuck her tongue out and made a face. "Well, that just means you have to find a hot guy to spend all your time with."

Lydia winked at her, and Trihn's mind immediately went to Preston. It wasn't as if he were the only guy in the city she would be interested in. He was just the most relevant at the current moment.

I do have his number. Maybe I should try to reach out to him...

"Maybe, Lydia."

"Maybe, maybe. Always maybe, baby. You need to get out more and date," Lydia said. She plopped down onto the bed next to Trihn and started braiding her hair without asking if it was all right.

"Speaking of, did you want to go to a party this weekend after I get out of rehearsal?"

"Oh! A party? What kind of party?" Lydia asked.

"Just some of my friends getting together."

"High school friends?" She sounded dismayed.

"Don't you know me better than that?"

"Model party?" she guessed.

"Only the best. Some people I know from London who I worked with last summer are going to be in town."

"Any hot guys?"

"What part of *models* did you not understand?" Trihn joked.

Not that models were Trihn's type. They were extremely good-looking, but so many of them were narcissistic to a fault. She couldn't handle a guy who took longer to get ready and had more hair products than her.

"Okay, I'm in. Can't pass up on hot models. Though…you're the one who shouldn't be passing up on hot models. You're too serious, and you need to loosen up."

Trihn rolled her eyes and stood. "I'm going to get my bag and get ready for dance."

"You can ignore me all you like, but you need a good lay," Lydia called loudly as Trihn walked out of the room.

She retreated to the shared bathroom and pulled on her tights and leotard under her ensemble. She forced all of her hair up into a high ponytail on top of her head and then removed her box of bobby pins. It took fifty of them to get all her hair up into a proper ballet bun. There was just too much hair for it to cooperate with fewer pins. She sprayed back the wisps around her face. After retouching her blush and mascara, she exited the bathroom and returned to Lydia, who continued to rant about how Trihn was too serious.

"Give it a rest, Ly!" Trihn said in exasperation. "I'm not you. I'm never going to be you."

"I'm not saying that you have to be!" Lydia cried. "I'm just saying that there's nothing *wrong* with casual sex."

Trihn shook her head. "I don't think there's anything *wrong* with it. Feel free to fuck around with whoever you want."

"I will."

"Good." Trihn hauled her bag onto her shoulder and slid into her heels. "I'm going to dance."

"Hey, don't be upset," Lydia said, following her to the front door.

"I'm not upset."

"You're clearly upset. I'm your sister. I should know."

Trihn let out a deep breath. Lydia could push her buttons like no one else. Trihn loved her sister to pieces, but the subject was already a sore one at the moment. It hadn't helped anything that Lydia was pushing.

"Just say you'll *think* about finding a nice guy to occupy your time this summer. You deserve it for all your hard work," Lydia said.

"I'm not dating someone or fucking someone as a prize for my accomplishments," Trihn said in frustration. "I want to date someone because I like him, because I could fall in love with him. I want to be with someone who I could marry."

Lydia's eyes widened. "You're eighteen years old, Trihn. Life isn't that serious. You don't have to marry anyone for a while, and if you keep talking like that, you're going to give me gray hair."

Trihn rolled her eyes. "You're insane."

"Probably, but creativity stems from madness. Or does madness stem from creativity?" she pondered. "Anyway, go to dance. Don't worry about finding someone to marry or whatever horrible thoughts are floating through your head. You're young and beautiful, and you should have so much more fun before you get married. This weekend, we'll find someone fun for you!"

"Okay, Lydia," Trihn said. If she didn't relent, Lydia would continue with her relentless diatribe.

What she didn't say was that she'd had *plenty* of that kind of fun during the past two years.

Lydia thought she was older and wiser; thus, she would be the one to corrupt her younger sister. But the truth was, with all the modeling events Trihn had been to, it had been almost too easy to be casual.

Now that she wasn't modeling, she was intent on finding something more meaningful.

THREE

A WEEK HAD PASSED BY IN THE BLINK OF AN EYE.

Trihn sank down to the floor of the dance studio and started working at the knots on the ribbons of her pointe shoes. She had just spent six long hours rehearsing for the Senior Showcase at the NYC Dance House this upcoming weekend. Her feet were killing her, and she had worn through *another* pair of shoes. At this rate, she would go through at least two more pairs before the performances and probably one each night next weekend during the shows.

Renée flexed her feet and then pushed up onto the toes of her shoes. "Do you see this shit?" Renée asked.

She moved up and down on her shoes, and Trihn could see that the hard insole of the shoes—normally, a perfect curve to her friend's foot—had split in half.

"The shank is completely broken. Fucking hell."

"Mine, too."

"What the hell am I going to do? I can't keep spitting out seventy-five dollars every week. I'm not made of money."

"We'll work it out. We always do."

Renée plopped down next to her and mercilessly tore at her shoes. "This wouldn't have happened if I wasn't in the middle of the fucking Intensive as well."

Trihn laughed. "My shoes are falling apart, and I'm not doing Intensive."

Every year, the NYC Dance House would put on a big summer dance workshop called The House Intensive. Dancers from all over the country would come to their studio to compete for dance scholarships. Renée was a scholarship recipient, so her participation in the summer program was required. The studio liked to showcase their prodigies. It helped that Renée had just been admitted into Juilliard for the fall. It was an incredible achievement for anyone but even more so for an African American scholarship student from the Bronx.

"Well, you should be helping with Intensive! There are so many fucking kids, and we need more brilliant-minded choreographers."

"Ha! You must be joking. We all know that I'm not a choreographer."

Renée gave her the look. She tilted her head down, cocked one eyebrow, and pursed her lips. "Puh-lease. I know what you do on your days off. That freestyle shit works in contemporary, too."

"That's why, in a week's time, I'm performing my senior piece in contemporary and then spending the rest of my summer doing what I do on my days off!"

"Whatever, hooker," Renée joked.

Trihn shook her head. It wasn't the first time she'd heard that one. "I just like to have a good time. Why don't you come with me tonight?" Trihn asked.

She shoved her shoes in her bag, and they headed to the dressing rooms.

"As much as I'd love to, I can't. My mom's expecting me home to watch the boys while she takes the night shift," Renée explained.

"What is she going to do when you're out of the house next year?" Trihn asked.

Renée sighed heavily. The choice to move to Manhattan and pursue her dreams had been really tough on Renée. Outside of dance, she'd work her butt off around the house while her mom worked three jobs to try to support their family.

"I try not to think about it. One day at a time," Renée said. "At least Matthew will be there to help tonight."

"Oh, I see how it is. You're really going home to be with the BF."

Matthew was Renée's boyfriend of three years. They were pretty much the cutest couple around. He was a jazz musician and swore up and down that he was going to compose a ballet for Renée like nothing anyone had ever seen before.

"Whatever," Renée cried.

Trihn stepped into a shower stall, peeled off her sweat-soaked tights and leotard, and stuffed them into an empty side pocket of her bag. She turned on the water and hurried under the spray when it was steaming hot. Her hair was still tightly held in its bun. She wouldn't have time to blow it out before meeting her friends. After washing off the hours of practice,

17

Trihn dried off and changed into a pair of tight leather booty shorts and a low-cut V-neck tank before slipping into her favorite pair of heels.

When she stepped back out, Renée just shook her head. "There's my hooker. Are you man-hunting tonight?"

"Yeah, right. You know me."

"Reconsider it. You look hot and could have any guy you wanted."

Trihn shrugged. "Maybe," she said, giving the same answer she had given Lydia.

When they had gone out last weekend, Lydia had ended up making out with two different male models who were out with them. Trihn had left empty-handed—again.

They hurried down the three flights of stairs and into the marble-tiled entryway. The revolving door was already locked tight for the night, and all but one light had been left on. The rest of the girls had left the building as soon as they could. Some of the management was still upstairs, but otherwise, it was dead.

"Do you want me to walk with you?" Renée asked.

"No. Don't worry about me. I'll catch a cab. Get home to your mom."

"I'm not looking forward to telling her about the shoes," she said softly.

Trihn grabbed her hand and stopped her before they exited. "I'll cover it if I have to. It's only one more week."

"Thanks, Trihn."

"What are friends for?"

They stepped out of the building and onto the brightly lit street. Even at eleven at night, people were still strolling the streets, and the sight made Trihn smile. She would never get tired of watching the way her city operated. It was home.

Trihn threw her hand out, and a cab pulled up to the curb. "You take this one," Trihn told her. She opened the back door and pushed her best friend toward it.

"No! You take it. You have to meet people!"

"I'll make it. You have farther to go."

Renée sighed. She could see that she was going to lose the argument, and the cab would leave them if one of them didn't get in. "Okay, but be careful."

"I always am," Trihn said.

She kissed Renée on the cheek, and then after she climbed into the backseat, Trihn shut the door behind her. The car drove off, and she searched for the next cab.

"How's the shoulder?"

Trihn whirled around in a panic. Her stomach leaped up into her throat. "Jesus!" she cried when she saw who it was. "Don't sneak up on people like that."

Preston smiled and held up his hands. "Sorry about that. Can't seem to get my footing with you."

"How the hell did you even know I would be here?" she asked suspiciously.

It was kind of creepy, having him show up outside the studio at the *exact* time that she had finished with dance. *How did he even know that I dance here?* It was probably about time to get into a cab or else she wouldn't be heeding Renée's advice to be careful.

She hedged backward a step.

19

"I saw your dance bag that day we ran into each other. I was in the neighborhood and thought I would just swing by," he clarified.

"At eleven o'clock at night?"

"Okay," he said with a nervous laugh. "You caught me. I actually asked around to see when your class would end, so I could surprise you."

"You have my phone number. Why didn't you just call?"

"Can't a guy surprise a girl anymore?"

Trihn raised her eyebrows. "Probably not at eleven at night after staking out her studio."

He ran a hand back through his messy blond hair and looked at his feet. This wasn't going at all the way he had planned it. She figured he had wanted to surprise her and have her think it was cute. And while she couldn't deny that her heart was beating wildly in her chest at the thought that he had stood out here, waiting just for her, she wasn't an idiot and didn't want to end up on a Missing Person poster.

"All right. My bad. I guess...I'll just head out. I didn't mean to freak you out," he apologized.

He shoved his hands down into the pockets of his dark jeans, bunching his black T-shirt up around his muscles and drawing her eyes to his body. He looked back up at her then with those sexy blue eyes, and her stomach dropped out of her body.

"Wait," she said before he could walk away. "I was just surprised. Why did you really show up anyway?"

"I wanted to check on your shoulder," he offered.

She rolled it twice. "It was a minor thing. Went away before dance last week."

"Oh. Oh, okay. Good."

He smiled again like he might just leave it at that, and in that moment, she decided that she couldn't let it end. He was undeniably attractive. He had sought her out at dance. There was no way she was just going to let him walk away again. She had been kicking herself for letting it happen in the first place.

"You have plans?" she asked.

"Have something in mind?" He took a step closer to her.

Her body heated at his nearness. Dear God, he was going to be the death of her.

"I'm meeting some friends. You could join...if you wanted," she offered.

"What am I in for?"

She shrugged, all nonchalant. "Just a regular night in New York City."

He laughed, and it was beautifully effortless. "This should be interesting."

FOUR

IT WAS NOT A NORMAL NIGHT IN THE CITY.

It never was when she had friends in town.

And it definitely was not going to be a normal night with Preston seated next to her in the cab on their way to the Meatpacking District.

She couldn't keep from stealing glances at him. Mostly, it was because she couldn't figure out how she had gotten up the nerve to invite him along. She never brought guys to these kinds of events. Plenty of other models would bring dates, but that just wasn't her. But these were her people, and the only other people she wanted associating with them were family and friends, like Lydia and Renée.

Yet she was about to throw Preston into the middle of this. *What the hell am I doing?*

The cab stopped at the corner of a large brick building, and before she could do anything, Preston paid for the trip.

"Thank you," she said as she got out of the car.

"Don't worry about it." His smile was genuine when he exited behind her. "Are you going to tell me what I'm walking into?"

"I have some friends in town. They're throwing a little…party." She cocked her head to the side and tried not to smile too broadly.

"A house party?" he asked dubiously.

"More like a…work party," she confided. She opened a heavy metal door. "Coming?"

He followed along, clearly intrigued. "And where do you work? The studio?"

She shook her head. "No, I just dance at the studio. I don't work anywhere right now. I kind of quit."

"And you still decided to come to the party?" His eyes widened in disbelief.

"It was an amicable break."

In truth, it was only *sort of* amicable. She had quit modeling because she was going to college. She had always seen school as a priority as a forward-thinking woman who wanted to make a splash in the world and prove her worth.

He laughed. "Publishing is not like that."

"You work in publishing?" she asked as they started up the rickety old stairs that creaked under their steps, bringing a smile to her face.

"Yeah, I'm an intern in the marketing department of *Glitz* magazine."

Trihn stumbled on the next step and had to catch herself on the railing. Preston reached out to steady her, but she waved him off.

"*Glitz* magazine?" she asked.

He ducked his chin to his chest, embarrassed. "Yeah. I know it's a fashion magazine, but internships are hard to come by in publishing, especially while I'm still in school."

He sounded like he had given this same speech many times, as if he were used to being judged as a man working for a high-end fashion magazine. Well, she didn't care that he worked for *Glitz*. In fact, her feminist ideals were screaming with joy at the knowledge. The fashion industry should be more balanced between men and women, especially in the world of fashion and beauty publishing.

However, the real reason she had stumbled was because her *mother* worked for *Glitz* magazine. It felt strangely coincidental, and she almost jotted out a text to ask if her mother had purposely put Preston in her path. She wouldn't put it past her mother. Like Lydia, she believed Trihn was too serious for her age. You would think that she would want at least one daughter to behave.

But looking up at Preston's concerned face changed Trihn's mind. She was just being jumpy. The likelihood that her mother had put him up to this was abysmally low. Her mother probably didn't even know anyone in the marketing department. She was certainly too high up on the food chain to notice a guy in an entry-level position.

Trihn probably should tell him that her mom worked there, but she kind of wanted to have him all to herself in that moment. She had just met him really. Revealing that her mom was a higher-up at the magazine he worked at would not be a good idea. Either he'd freak out or want to somehow use her to move up in the company.

God, she was having negative thoughts. She just wanted this one night to herself without anyone else's expectations looming over her.

Trihn held her hand up to stop him from continuing. "You don't have to explain. I get it. Everyone has to start somewhere."

"Right," he agreed. He seemed pleased that she hadn't questioned him. "So, where did you start?"

She raised her eyebrow. "You'll see."

They had reached their floor, and she walked him over to the door that led to the party. She knocked twice, and then the door opened. A familiar face smiled back at her.

"Trihn!" Francesca cried. "I knew you couldn't resist us!"

"Of course I couldn't," she said. Trihn enveloped the woman in a hug, knowing that she wasn't the hugging type.

Francesca patted her on the back. When she saw Trihn had someone with her, her eyes widened. "Well, well, who do we have here?"

Preston turned into a perfect gentleman in the blink of an eye. He straightened, becoming markedly taller than Francesca's six-foot-tall frame, and stuck his hand out. "Nice to meet you. I'm Preston Whitehall."

She lightly took his hand in hers and winked. "Oh, the pleasure is all mine. And you can call me whatever you'd like. I don't discriminate with someone who has a body like this."

Trihn buried her head in her hands. "He's here with me, Francesca."

"Oh, dear!" she said, removing her hand. "I thought you'd brought me a present."

"Not tonight, I'm afraid," Trihn said.

"Well, come in, and enjoy the party. Tell me everything! We've missed you."

Trihn and Preston crossed the threshold into a massive open studio with floor-to-ceiling glass windows across one entire wall. Large wooden beams crisscrossed the ceiling, and huge white columns were interspersed across the antique hardwood floor. Everything was white and cheery and full of beautiful people.

"A studio party?" Preston asked curiously, taking in their surroundings. He gave her a serious side eye. "What kind of work were you in exactly?"

Francesca derisively arched a perfectly manicured eyebrow and flipped her stick-straight blonde hair over her shoulder. "Surely you know how talented our little Trihn is. She could have been a superstar if she had just forgotten this silly idea about going to university." Her South African accent became more prominent the longer she spoke to Preston.

Trihn had to hide her embarrassment at Francesca's words.

"Please, feel free to enlighten me."

He crossed his arms over his chest, and Trihn couldn't help but stare. Even though gorgeous people surrounded them, her eyes were only for him and the very sexy muscles in his arms.

Whoa! Arms. She should stop staring at those arms.

She looked back up into his eyes and could feel a blush touching her cheeks. For once, she was happy for her mixed Vietnamese and Brazilian ancestry that hid the red on her cheeks.

"He knows nothing?" Francesca asked Trihn.

"I wanted it to be a surprise."

"A surprise indeed," she trilled. "We just wrapped up a modeling shoot this afternoon for Gucci. Perhaps you've heard of the designer. Now, we're toasting our last night in New York before I begin on a new grand adventure that I'll have to tell you all about later."

"Gucci?" Preston's eyes widened.

"Yep," Trihn agreed. "I worked for them on their summer line. The shoot today was for their fall line."

"That unfortunately you were not a part of," Francesca chastised.

"You're a model?" Preston asked Trihn, as if he didn't have the proof right before his eyes.

"I *was* a model," Trihn corrected him.

"I would never have pegged you for a model."

"What does *that* mean?" she asked indignantly.

"That's not what I meant," he said quickly. "You're beautiful. Of course you could model."

Trihn felt her body coiling into a knot of tension. *Beautiful, of course*—she hadn't needed those words from him. She knew that it wasn't an insult. It was anything but an insult. However, everyone said she was beautiful. The term was almost an afterthought. But she hated the idea of anyone saying she couldn't do something she'd put her mind to.

"I guess I've only seen the ballerina," he confessed.

"Well, look closer," Francesca said. She pointed to Trihn's feet. "Those are Christian Louboutin. No satin-toe shoes for her."

"So they are." He wasn't looking at her shoes though. His eyes were transfixed on her face. "Seems I have a lot to learn about you."

Trihn laughed, trying to brush aside the butterflies in her stomach at the mention of him wanting to get to know her—not to mention, that look…like he wanted to eat her right up. "Well, we have all night."

"So we do." With the way he'd said it, the words took on a whole new meaning.

"Come on, lovebirds, let's get drinks," Francesca said, guiding them across the room.

She busied herself with introducing them to everyone as they traversed the room. Preston smiled and nodded, as if he were going to remember any of the people they'd passed.

Trihn started whispering into his ear the name of the countries the people were from, "Australia. Brazil. California."

"California isn't a country."

She laughed. "It might as well be if you're from New York."

He guffawed at her comment and covered it by putting his hand on the small of her back, directing her toward the drinks. "Excuse me, California," he said with a completely straight face to the busty blonde model in front of them.

"Oh my gosh, you did not just call her California. Do you know who that is?"

He shook his head. "The only person in this room I care about is you," he breathed into her ear.

Trihn shivered against his touch. *Well, this is off to a good start.*

She was an idiot for not calling him. He was hot and smart and caring. He worked in publishing—in her industry, no less. Plus, those arms and lips and smile and—

Preston passed her a glass of wine, and he took a beer from the bartender. Then, they milled around the room, talking to people she had worked for earlier this year. It was easy to move back into the swing of things with these people, even with Preston at her side. She had never thought it would be this seamless, but Preston fit right in.

By the end of the night, her girlfriends were enamored with him, the guys were asking him about his workout regimen and promising to get together for gym dates—which she assured him was not entirely what he was thinking—and Trihn found herself completely in thrall with him.

He took her by the hand and pulled her out onto the mostly empty balcony. He twirled her around in place. She laughed and rose onto her tiptoes, spinning in place like a perfect ballerina, before being drawn into his arms.

"This was fun. You seemed worried at first," he told her.

"I've never brought anyone to a model event with me besides my sister and my best friend," she confessed.

"I'm honored," he said, leaning his head against her forehead.

A spark ignited in her stomach as she swam in the sea of blue before her.

Everything narrowed down to this one moment—the look in his eyes, the feel of his hands sneaking under her shirt and grasping her skin, the energy igniting between them, their breaths intermingling in the small distance separating their bodies.

She felt herself freeze.

This wasn't some fling that she would cast aside for the next hottie at a different shoot. This wasn't some guy she'd make out with in a club after a good drink. This wasn't a mistake.

This felt right, inexplicably right, in a way she had never felt before.

Their noses touched. She slid her hands up around his neck, drawing him closer. She wanted this. It wasn't because she was listening to everyone around her, telling her to have a good time, to let herself get lost in something, not to be serious. It was because he made her serious nature seem normal. He made her feel...

That was enough for now. It didn't have to be more. Just the promise of a beginning.

Their lips slid together, and the entire world disappeared completely, utterly falling away into some other universe. Her heart rushed into her throat, and her whole body contracted at the feel of him pressing against her. His tongue slipped invitingly against her bottom lip, and she opened the invitation with zeal, meeting him halfway. They moved against each other with practiced ease. Her whole body trembled with the heat and desire coursing through her.

Right then, she had never wanted anything more than this kiss. It was both tempting and terrifying because she felt as if she would give up everything to have this again.

As he leaned her against the railing, promising her the world with this kiss, the biggest cost she worried about was her heart.

FIVE

"WHAT DO YOU MEAN, you don't like peanut butter?" Preston asked a week and a half later.

They both stared into the glass counter filled with an array of gorgeous pastries of every variety—cupcakes, cake, macarons, tarts, cheesecake, cookies. The list was endless.

"I don't like it," she told him. "I never have."

"I can't comprehend this."

She laughed and shrugged her shoulders. "It's gross. I don't even like the smell. So, if you think that I'm going to kiss you after you eat that, you're crazy."

He took the peanut butter–chocolate chip cupcake on a small paper plate from the woman and gave Trihn puppy-dog eyes. "I bet I could convince you otherwise."

"No way." Trihn wrinkled her nose.

"I have my ways."

She laughed lightly and then spoke to the employee, "I'll take a mocha fudge cupcake, please."

She was handed her cupcake as well, and then they went to the register. Preston insisted on paying for the treats. He grabbed two plastic forks, and then they walked outside to find a bench to indulge themselves.

"Even though you hate my choice in dessert," he said, pretending to be wounded, "this is for you. Congrats on your dance performance last night. I only wish that I could have been there to see it."

Preston toasted Trihn with his cupcake, and they both dug in.

Following the model party, she had invited Preston to her Senior Showcase. She hadn't expected him to be interested in seeing her dance, and she hated admitting that she had been disappointed that he couldn't come last weekend. But it was just as unexpected that he was doing something like this for her when he hadn't been able to make it.

"I would have liked for you to have been there, too," she told him after she finished off her cupcake.

"If only I wasn't such an overachiever, then I could have made it."

She held her hand up. "Overachieving, I am *very* familiar with."

"The model ballerina?" he asked skeptically.

"Hey now! Modeling and ballet, dance in general, are very strenuous. Anyway, I'm quitting both to pursue a degree in fashion design at one of the best schools in the country." She didn't mention how much it pained her to give them up, but it was the right thing to do. She needed to focus on her education to get the kind of job she had always dreamed bout.

"While I'm glad you're coming to NYU, why does it sound like that's not what you want?"

She sighed heavily and avoided his knowing blue gaze. He was seeing right through her bravado.

"It's not that. I guess I just always thought that dance would be a part of my life. I've only been modeling for three years, but it also kind of seemed like something I wouldn't stop until I was too old for the market," she said with a sad smile.

"Then, why stop?" he asked, his cupcake forgotten.

"I don't *want* to stop, but I'll need to take my studies seriously. I need to place at the top of the fashion design program. I want to design for Bergdorf Goodman and open my own boutique on Fifth Avenue. I can't do those things and—"

"Have a life?" he ventured.

"Exactly."

"You sound like you put way too much pressure on yourself."

She shrugged. "Maybe, but it was how I was raised. Plus, my sister is a mega genius, one of those people who doesn't have to try at anything. Hard to live up to that."

Preston bridged the distance between them and laced their fingers together. "You don't have to live up to anyone. Just look at you. You're gorgeous and smart and driven, and you seem pretty awesome to me."

Her cheeks heated. "You've only known me for a week."

"And I've seen all of that in a week," he said confidently.

"Well, thank you."

"My father works in investing," he said after a silent minute. "He always expected me to do something like that. One day, I just decided that it wasn't for me. I don't ever want to do something for expectations. I want to earn my place in life because it's what *I* want, not what someone else wants. He wasn't exactly happy that I'd started working for a fashion magazine. But I think he's going to come around and realize that I go after what I want." He purposefully looked up at her. "And when I have my mind set on something, I'll do anything to keep it."

Trihn bit her lip. "Why do I feel like we're not talking about work anymore?"

"Because we're not."

Then, he kissed her.

It didn't matter that they were seated on the side of a crowded street in New York City, making a spectacle of themselves. All that was there in that moment was the feel of his lips on hers, the way her heart stuttered to life, and the dizzy feeling clouding her mind.

When he pulled back, he was smirking.

"What?" she asked, flustered.

"I told you I had my ways to get you to kiss me."

"You're lucky I like you," she told him with a shake of her head.

EMERALDS

*Are you still coming by for our afternoon
coffee? I have to get back upstairs soon.*

Trihn sighed heavily when she got the text message
from Preston. She'd had every intention of meeting
up with him for coffee after his meeting with his
boss, but Lydia was taking forever. Trihn had agreed
to have lunch with her sister since her plans with
Preston had been disrupted. It wasn't often that Lydia
had lunch open at a decent time with her new job
anyway. Trihn had thought it would be easy to juggle
both, but she hadn't told Lydia about Preston yet, so
she couldn't exactly rush her without raising
suspicion.

Lydia finally put her fork down and called for a
waiter to bring them a check. Trihn breathed out in
relief. She might still make it.

*Yes. Just finishing up lunch with
my sister. Sorry.*

Lydia put her credit card in the black booklet.

Trihn tried to stop her. "Ly, you seriously don't
have to pay for my lunch." She furtively glanced
down at her phone to check the time…again.

"Don't worry about it. I can see you're in a
hurry."

"What?" Trihn asked, looking up. "No, I'm not."

"Well, if you aren't, then you're acting really
weird."

"I'm not acting weird either."

Lydia snorted. "Okay."

Trihn's phone beeped again.

No worries. Just wanted to see you.

"So," Lydia said, "who is he?"

"Who is whom?" she asked.

Her eyes met her sister's across the table. Lydia gave her an all-knowing look.

"It's just Renée."

"Uh-huh." Lydia rolled her eyes. "I got the check. You run along and tell me about him later."

Trihn stood up from her seat and shook her head. "Seriously, it's no one."

"You act as if I don't know my sister."

"I love you, Ly," Trihn said. She kissed the top of her sister's head and then began jogging out of the restaurant.

"I want the dirt later," Lydia cried as she left.

Trihn hopped on the subway and took the train uptown to Preston's building. Trihn had been to *Glitz* magazine headquarters more times than she could count throughout the last eight years since her mother had become the executive vice president of the company. It was strange, being on her way there for something…someone else.

She jogged to get there in time, and she was thankful that she had opted for her studded gold flats. Pedestrians gave her evil glares when they managed to look up from their cell phones.

And there he was, waiting for her in a crisp black suit.

A smile plastered itself onto her face at the sight of his dark blond hair and characteristic smirk.

His eyes found her across the short distance on the sidewalk, and he moved toward her like a magnet. "Hey, beautiful."

"Hey," she whispered.

His hands fell to either side of her face, and he softly kissed her on the lips. It was intoxicating. She could do this all day. Her stomach dropped out from under her. All she could do was clutch on to him and hope that she would stay standing, despite the fact that he was turning her legs to mush.

He broke the spell and gestured for them to walk into the Starbucks inside the building.

"Sorry about lunch. I thought we would be done sooner," she told him.

"That's all right. Just trying to steal more of your time."

"I don't mind that at all."

He charmingly smiled down at her, and she felt that now familiar flutter in her stomach. She had to force herself to look away to avoid getting completely blinded by him.

They ordered their drinks, picked them up from the barista, and then walked back into the building. Trihn stealthily looked around the lobby. The last thing she wanted was to run into her mother. She rarely took lunch out unless she had important meetings, but it still made Trihn cautious.

Preston put his free arm around her waist and leaned into her. "Don't make plans for lunch tomorrow."

"I'm all yours."

"I like the sound of that." He dragged her against him for another heart-stopping kiss. "I'm not ready for you to leave. Come up, and see the office."

"Are you sure? Don't you have to get back to work?"

"Of course I'm sure. It'll only be a minute."

"All right. Then, yes!"

Trihn followed him to the elevators. She was excited to see where he spent much of his life. If he wasn't with her, then he was guaranteed to be working. She was glad that they had started having lunch together nearly every day because most of his nights were occupied. He took *overachiever* to a whole new level.

The elevator opened onto his floor, and Preston whisked them by an oblivious receptionist. He walked Trihn past a giant wall with the *Glitz* magazine logo and into the immaculate office space beyond. Nearly every space was occupied with white cubicles. Most of them were empty from the lunch hour, and only a few people had trickled back in already. All-glass meeting rooms were in use across one far wall, and the other wall opened up to the New York City skyline beyond.

"And this," he said dramatically, "is my desk."

Trihn giggled. It looked just like every other cubicle on the floor. "Very nice."

"Seriously, this is where the magic happens."

"I like it."

"One day, I'll be up there," he said, plopping down into his seat.

"In the sky?" she joked.

"With the bigwigs, making the decisions."

Trihn bit her lip. "Very ambitious of you."

"You sound disbelieving."

"I'm not," she said earnestly. "If I can become a successful fashion designer, then why can't you run a fashion magazine?"

He smiled in a way that said she completely understood. And she did. She knew what it felt like to want to make it to the top. She had felt that all her life. Between ballet, modeling, Lydia…all she had ever done was strive to be the best.

Preston grabbed her hand and pulled her down onto his lap. His hands circled her waist as he stared up at her. "You get it."

"I get that you'd give my designs all the best placements in the magazine," she joked to defuse the heat radiating between them.

"Oh, you think you'd get special treatment, do you?" he asked.

He trailed a row of soft kisses down her neck, and she shivered all over.

"Absolutely."

"You might just be right." He nipped her neck.

Her shivers turned into a full-blown shudder at his touch. She turned her face toward him, and their lips met. His tongue slid into her mouth, and her hands wrapped around his neck. Where they were and what they were doing didn't seem to matter at that moment.

Then, someone cleared his throat behind them. "Well, what do we have here?"

Trihn jumped up like a shot of electricity had rushed through her. "I'm so sorry," she apologized immediately.

Preston stood hastily and brushed down his suit. "Sorry about that, Mr. Brown."

Crap. His boss.

"I was just leaving," Trihn said awkwardly.

"Perhaps Mr. Whitehall can escort you out, as he should have earlier."

"Yes, sir," Preston said quickly.

Trihn hastened her steps back toward the elevators with Preston on her heels. She stared down at her feet as she waited for the door to open. "Sorry. I didn't mean to get you in trouble with your boss."

"Hey," he said, tilting her chin up, "I'm not in trouble. Even if I were, it would be worth it to have a few extra minutes with you."

She couldn't help the smile from blossoming on her face.

"Lunch tomorrow?" he asked.

"I wouldn't miss it."

SIX

THE LAST FEW WEEKS had been a blur of Preston.

Trihn had been spending more time in Manhattan than she'd ever had before in her life. Despite Renée's requests for her help with Intensive, she had been using her new free time to be with Preston. He had work, of course, and she still had to go home at night to Brooklyn, or her parents would freak out. They had already been asking questions about her being gone so much. Leave it to her parents to get overly sentimental about her moving into the city before it even happened.

Even though she'd been with Preston a lot, she didn't feel overwhelmed like she'd thought she might. In fact, she became more excited each time. She had never felt like this before. Her insides would turn to Jell-O when she saw his name on her cell phone.

She'd swoon at the thought of meeting him after work. Her head would feel light at the prospect of kissing him...of doing much, much more than that.

Things she was clearly ready for.

Very ready for.

Things she was hoping would happen tonight.

"How do I look?" Trihn asked Lydia, coming out of her sister's bathroom.

She had taken way too long in deciding on what to wear tonight and finally ended up on an emerald-green dress that matched her eyes. It hugged her figure like a glove and stopped at mid-thigh. She paired it with nude heels and light jewelry. Her makeup enhanced her beauty, giving her cat eyes and high cheekbones.

"Like you have a date," Lydia said. She sat up straight on the bed.

"Well, I do."

"A date you're excited for."

"I am." She bit her lip. "Can you tell Mom and Dad, if they ask, that I'm staying with you tonight?"

"Oh my God!" Lydia shot up off the bed and jumped up and down. "This is so exciting. Who is this guy?"

"No one. I don't want it to be a big deal. We're not serious or anything."

"You're serious enough for a date in *that*! This is all-new territory for you!"

"This is the reason I haven't told you," Trihn said.

"Because I'd be excited for you?" Lydia looked at her in dismay.

"No, because you'd make me feel like a freak for not having gone on a real date like this before."

Lydia rolled her eyes. "Whatever. You're not a freak. You're just…picky. But who cares? I'm happy for you. When do I get to meet him?"

"How about never?" Trihn said immediately.

"I don't bite!" she cried. "Plus, I have to approve of him."

"I don't need your approval. It's too new, Ly. I don't want to scare him off."

"I won't scare him! I'll be a perfect big sister."

Trihn rolled her eyes. *Yeah, right.* "Give me the summer. Then, if this is still the real deal when I start school in the fall, then you can meet him."

"That's, like…six weeks away," she complained.

"Less than six weeks away. Now, hand me my purse, so I can head out of here."

Lydia pouted but handed over the black clutch. Trihn kissed her on the cheek before leaving the apartment. She hailed a cab to Preston's apartment, and when she landed on the sidewalk outside his place, she shifted anxiously from foot to foot.

Preston came out of the door of his apartment building a minute later. She launched herself at him without a thought, and he chuckled into her ear, holding her tight against him.

"Hey, beautiful," he whispered.

"I missed you."

He kissed the top of her head and squeezed her a little bit harder. "I missed you, too. Are you ready to go?"

"Yeah. Are you going to tell me where we're going?" she asked.

"You'll see."

"Oh, I see how it's going to be. Trying to keep secrets," she joked.

He raised his eyebrows. "I don't want to hear it. You walked me into a model studio party with a hundred beautiful people without warning."

"I probably should have warned you, considering the number of people who hit on you."

"The only people in that room who hit on me were men," he confessed, shaking his head and leaning out to hail a cab.

"Wait! What about me?" she asked with a pout.

"Were you hitting on me? I didn't notice."

She smacked him on the arm. "I think you noticed. You were making out with me at the end of the night."

He pulled open the cab door, and as she slid by him into the backseat, he gasped lightly in surprise. "Was that you?"

Trihn shook her head in exasperation. Only this man could tease her like this without her strangling him. "Let me remind you," she said.

When he sat down, she drew him in for a kiss. He tasted like cinnamon candy, and she just wanted to eat him right up. Their lips melded together, and she felt the world drop away, as it only could with him touching her.

Then, the cab driver cussed loudly, interrupting them, and Trihn pulled away, embarrassed. "Where are you headed? I don't have all day."

"Sorry," Preston said quickly. "Lincoln Center."

Her head snapped to the side. "What?"

"Ever been before?" he asked coyly.

"Are you kidding me? Do you know how many times I've been to Lincoln Center? I'm in love with The Metropolitan Opera House. My best friend just got into Juilliard."

"Well, I thought this might be up your alley."

He retrieved a pair of tickets from the inside pocket of his suit coat and handed them to her. She stared down at the tickets with delight. Preston was taking her to the ballet to see *Giselle*. It was one of her favorites, too.

"Thank you." She beamed up at him and threaded their fingers together.

He gave her another deep kiss. "Only the best for you."

The drive Uptown was surprisingly easy, and they made it to Lincoln Center with plenty of time to find their seats inside the theater. They were about midway back on the orchestra level, on the aisle. Preston took the inner seat so that she would have the best view of the stage.

Excitement was already coursing through her body at what she was about to see. She had seen many ballets, but each time it was as if she couldn't breathe when watching. She could judge their movements, the precision behind their leaps and turns, and the extension of the men and women onstage, but all of that would seem to blur. She would just get lost in the dance. That was all that mattered.

The lights dimmed, everyone rushed to get to their seats, and then the curtain rose, transporting the audience into another world.

Trihn sank back into her seat just as the first ballerina floated onto the stage. As she reveled in the performance, Preston ran his hand up her arm and to her shoulder, sending shivers down her spine. She glanced over at him, and he had this dirty smirk on his face. He wasn't even watching the ballet. His eyes were solely trained on her.

She swallowed and stared forward, but her attention was torn. His fingers brushed her long tresses off her neck. The palm of his hand pushed flat against her skin and went up into her hair. He gently pulled it, and as her head dipped backward, her eyes closed of their own accord.

With his other hand, he laced their fingers together, bringing her hand to his lips. He tenderly kissed each knuckle before drawing her thumb between his teeth. She inhaled deeply.

He seemed to be enjoying himself as he kneaded the muscles in her neck. He leaned forward toward her and planted a soft kiss on her shoulder.

"Keep your eyes open. You don't want to miss a second of this," he breathed softly.

Dear God! He was teasing her. This was sweet, blissful torture.

She could hardly concentrate. Keeping up with two things at once, when one was tempting her with everything she wanted, was harder than it seemed. As the ballet drew to a close, she was glad that she had seen it before or else she would have been entirely lost as to what had happened during much of the performance.

His touch was captivating, and she found she was a lost cause when it came to this man. She hadn't just forgotten the ballet in front of her face. The world had disappeared all around her. In a sea of people, there was just him.

The curtain dropped unexpectedly, bright lights flooded the auditorium, and Trihn jolted upright. Preston sat up straight, as if he hadn't just been working her into a frenzy with the lightest touches imaginable. The smirk on his face was the only indication that anything was amiss.

As the curtain rose and the dancers began to take their bows, Trihn stood on shaky legs to give the ballet that she couldn't remember a standing ovation. Preston applauded at her side. They clapped until everyone left the stage, and people started filing out.

She exited into the aisle, and Preston grabbed her hand again.

"Hey, we're not done," he said. The words were suggestive and were accented by his hand squeezing around her waist.

"Oh?" she managed to get out.

"Come on. I think you'll like this surprise better."

"Why is that?" she asked.

"Because I'd like to finish what I started."

SEVEN

ALMOST EVERYONE HAD ABANDONED THE THEATER
by the time Preston and Trihn rounded the corner to
the backstage entrance.

"What are we doing?" she asked.

He flashed her a toothy grin before pulling out
two backstage Press passes.

Her eyes widened. "Where did you get those?"

"Work." He shrugged his shoulders, as if using
Press passes to get them backstage was totally normal.

"I don't think you're supposed to use them for
this," she whispered as they approached the door.

"Live a little with me."

She had no other choice. They were going to the
backstage area of The Metropolitan Opera House, a
stage she dreamed of performing on. She was excited
and decided she didn't care how he was about to use

Press passes. She wanted to go backstage…and she wanted Preston to keep his promise to finish what he had started during the ballet.

Preston flashed their passes to the older gentleman manning the door. He brightly smiled at them and gave them directions to where the interviews were being conducted. The man was so nice that it *almost* made Trihn feel bad.

Then, Preston grabbed her hand again and began pulling her down the hallway. She giggled and clutched on to his body.

She remained silent as they walked through mostly empty hallways. Preston had this thing down pat. In the midst of their deceit, she tried to mirror his confidence, acting as if they were supposed to be there.

He took a seemingly random turn, fiddled with the doorknob, and then pushed it open. "After you," he said.

Her eyes darted down the hallway. She was just waiting for someone to come out and notice what they were up to, but whatever was going on after the performance kept others far removed from this room. She entered with Preston on her heels. He shut the door behind her, casting them into darkness.

"I can't believe we're doing this," she whispered.

His hands grazed her sides. "What's the worst that could happen?"

"We get caught. They kick us out. Someone calls the police. We end up in jail!" she said dramatically.

"We'll just say we took a wrong turn." He kissed her exposed shoulder.

"They won't believe us."

"People believe anything you tell them with enough conviction."

"Is that so?"

"Yes. Like right now, I'm going to get you out of that dress that has been tempting me all evening."

He grabbed her waist and pushed her back against the door. She thudded noisily, and a giggle escaped her mouth. His lips found hers in the darkness, and suddenly, her arms were forced over her head. A groan escaped her mouth. She thrust her body hard against his, grinding her core against his suit pants.

He locked her wrists together over her head and then reached around to slide the zipper of her dress down. It hit the base of her spine, and then the material slid down her narrow hips to pool at her feet.

"See?" he teased.

"Doesn't count," she purred. "I wanted you to do that."

He nipped at her bottom lip. "I think you're going to want me to do everything else I'm about to do, too."

She had a feeling he was right.

Now that her eyes had adjusted to the sliver of light coming from the base of the door, she pulled back to get a good look at him. He was just staring at her, almost waiting for permission, which was something he plainly didn't need. Or maybe he just wanted to make sure she was okay. Normally, she would be drunk, and things would just…happen. It brought a smile to her lips that being with Preston was so different than her life before him.

Her smile must have been what he was looking for because, in that instant, everything shifted. The air between them heated and crackled. His mouth crashed down onto hers, and the world disappeared.

Whatever had been building between them during the performance, building between them for weeks, was crashing down all around them. She couldn't contain it, nor did she want to. She wanted him to take what was his. She wanted to be his fully and completely.

His hand left her wrists, and she dropped her hands to his shoulders, holding on to the stiff material of his jacket. He wrapped his arms around her and grabbed her ass in both hands. She gasped against his mouth. He took that as an opportunity to delve deeper with his tongue and dig deeper with his fingers.

Time seemed to stretch between them. They were in a hurry due to the circumstances of being locked in an empty room backstage, but still, he seemed to want to explore her body. His hands traveled over her waist, down the backs of her legs, and then up her inner thighs. She shuddered against him as she wrestled with unbuttoning his shirt and getting beneath it to his glorious abs. She started for his belt buckle without pause, but then everything came to a screeching halt when he touched her pulsing center.

"Oh God," she moaned softly, trying to keep her voice down.

Until that moment, she hadn't realized how much she'd truly wanted him. Her body was on fire, pulsing and radiating heat at his eager touch. His finger swirled around her clit through the soft material of her thong. She trembled, nearly coming undone right then and there.

"I like you like this."

"How?" she managed to get out.

"Powerless at my fingertips."

"I will be like this whenever you want me to."

He chuckled softly against her mouth and continued his work on her lower body. "I want to feel this," he said, slipping a digit under her thong and soaking his finger, "all around me."

"Oh, yes," she moaned.

At the feel of him, her body convulsed of its own will. She was so worked up that she could barely get her hands moving to undo his belt buckle, pop the button on his pants, and drop the zipper. She freed his cock from his boxers and gave it a few good strokes.

His head fell into the crook of her shoulder. "Fuck."

The way he'd drawled it out with a deep throaty moan as she grabbed his cock made *fuck* her new favorite word.

Preston roughly hoisted her up, so that her legs circled his waist, and then forced her back against the door. She held on to his shoulders for support and was glad for her dancer balance.

He yanked her underwear to the side, and their bodies moved together until the tip of his dick was positioned over her opening. He shifted up into her just an inch, and she tensed at the slight intrusion.

It had been…a long time since she had done this, and the first time hadn't been the best of experiences. She had promised herself that, when it happened again, it would be with the right person, for the right reasons. She had to remind herself that she had no reservations about Preston, and she forced herself to relax.

With ease, Preston pushed up into her slick wetness. Her head tipped back at the feel of him filling her, and she let loose a string of her new favorite word.

He chuckled hoarsely into her shoulder.

"You're...so—shit," he said incoherently. "Tight."

"Mmm," she groaned back.

He had stolen the rest of the words from her. Then, he started moving, and despite her loss of words, she found that she was loud enough anyway. He covered her mouth with a fierce kiss to try to silence her as he moved in and out. She pushed herself harder against him, meeting his movements as best as she could. His grip on her was firm as he did much of the directing, and she didn't mind at all.

A rustling outside the door made her head pop up, and her eyes widened in alarm. "Shit," she whispered.

Preston stopped abruptly and waited to hear what was going on. She could hear voices passing by the door, but she couldn't make out the sounds. More came and went, and Trihn wondered if the dancers were leaving the building. If they got stuck here, she had no idea what they were going to do.

"Maybe we should go," she hissed.

He gave her a disbelieving look. "Hell no."

"There are people out there!"

"They can wait," he said.

He started moving, and her body fired up all over again.

"Preston..." she pleaded, unsure of whether she was asking him to stop or start.

Her body was enjoying everything he was doing to her.

"They can wait, Trihn," he repeated quietly. "I have every intention of finishing you first."

And why would I keep him from that? She prayed no one would hear and that she could keep quiet, but he sure as hell was making that difficult.

The voices outside the room became louder and more frequent as his thrusts picked up pace. She bit her lip to keep from crying out and closed her eyes. Her body was humming. She could barely breathe. She could feel sweat beading on her brow. She couldn't hold back any longer.

She tightened around him, and then everything released all at once. Her body shook uncontrollably. It felt like a hurricane was ripping through her. And it was pure bliss.

He jerked inside her. His whole body was a knot of tension, and then a euphoric smile touched his lips as he finished. "You're…amazing," he drawled slowly.

He pulled back and let her legs drop to the ground. They were shaking from the energy it had taken to hold herself up. She was glad his muscular arms had carried much of her weight. As he righted himself, she pulled her dress on, leaned back against the door, and sighed heavily.

They waited until the voices outside the door disappeared before peeking around the corner and exiting as discreetly as possible. She tightly held his hand and avoided eye contact with anyone they passed. She was sure she looked mussed and freshly sexed. And she didn't care one bit.

They took a taxi back to his apartment. Before he had even gotten his front door closed, he was peeling her dress off again. She couldn't seem to get enough of him, and he couldn't seem to get enough of her. They fell into bed together.

It wasn't until several hours later that she finally laid her head against his bare chest and felt her body succumb to sleep. It was the first night she had ever stayed at a guy's place, and it couldn't have been more perfect.

EIGHT

"ARE YOU GOING INTO THE CITY AGAIN?" Trihn's mother, Linh, asked.

"Yep," Trihn said.

She grabbed a vegetarian roll off the tray her mother was preparing them on and stuffed it into her mouth. "Thanks," she said through a mouthful of food.

"Trihnity," she said, shaking her head, "don't you think you've been spending a lot of time in Manhattan?"

Trihn's phone dinged in the pocket of her ripped black skinny jeans, and she pulled it out. She ignored her mother's question. She was concerned. Trihn got it. She had heard it enough lately. Her mother had never cared that much before about her going into the city.

About ready to leave to go see Preston, she checked her new text message.

Got called into work. Hate having to cancel.

Damn.

No problem. Let me know if you can get away. xoxo

Will do.

"Trihn! Did you hear anything I just said?" Linh asked.

Her head popped up. "Was I supposed to be listening?"

"Your father will be back home tonight. Why don't you stay in and hang out with us before you leave for good?" she asked.

Trihn moved over to her mom and kissed her on the cheek. "I love you, but I promised I'd help Renée with Intensive," she ad-libbed. She hadn't planned to do that, but she didn't particularly want to stay in, wait, and wonder about Preston.

"If I didn't know better, I'd think a boy was involved."

"Nope, no boy."

Her mother gave her a long level look.

Trihn sighed heavily. "Ly told you, didn't she?"

"She loves you," Linh said in response.

Trihn snorted. Lydia liked to be the center of attention, and she and Mom had this older-sibling *bond* where they always ended up telling each other everything.

"So, who is he?" Linh asked, returning to making her lunch.

"Mom! I can't do this right now."

"I'm just asking," she said sympathetically. "You never date."

"I'm leaving now."

Trihn grabbed her dance bag out of the front closet and slipped into her favorite pair of combat boots. Linh followed her to the door.

"I'm not trying to badger you, but you shouldn't feel like you have to hide something like this from me. Lydia doesn't."

"I'm not Lydia, Mom."

"I never said you were." Linh held up her hands defensively. "But if you want to bring your young man over for dinner, I wouldn't object either."

Trihn rolled her eyes and opened the door. "He's not my young man. He's just a guy I've been seeing, and it's not a big deal, so please stop acting like it is. I have to go or else I'm going to be late."

She slung her bag over her shoulder and exited the house with her mother reminding her that she loved her. She trudged down the street and took her normal entrance to the subway, swiping her well-used pass, and slinking into her seat on the way into the city.

Her mother meant well, but Trihn wasn't about to scare Preston by bringing him home to meet the 'rents after only a couple of weeks. Only Lydia would be crazy enough to do something like that with her flavor-of-the-week boyfriend.

Trihn reached the studio right as the lunch hour ended for the Intensive students. She strolled upstairs with her hair still down in her most comfortable destroyed look, and she dropped the dance bag at Renée's feet.

"Hey, Teach," she joked.

Renée raised her eyebrows. "Who let this trash into my studio?"

Trihn laughed. "Miss me?"

"I knew you couldn't resist coming in," she quipped. "Now, go get in some real fucking clothes, and get to a barre."

For the most part, Trihn did as instructed. After changing, she spent the rest of the class helping Renée wrangle a group of teenagers before going through the barre exercises and spending a few hours working on the difficult choreography Renée had put together. It was exhausting and therapeutic. It had only been a few weeks since she stopped dancing, and already, her body had forgotten how rigorous it was. She had missed the constant ache of pushing her muscles to their limits.

When classes ended for the day, Renée sent them off to get dinner on their own before they headed back to the nearby dorms for the night. After a quick shower, Trihn and Renée went in search of dinner themselves.

"I'm glad you could drop by," Renée said once they were seated at a nearby diner. "I haven't seen you much, and I missed having you in class during the week."

"Me, too," Trihn said, realizing how true it was. Dance had been so central to her existence for so long. It was hard to think about what her life would be like without it.

"What have you been doing with all your time? Hanging out with Lydia? How does she like photographing for a magazine?" Renée asked. "I'd think her hippie sensibilities would take over and make her feel like a sellout."

Trihn laughed. "I think she's enjoying it actually. Even as some bullshit assistant to a second shooter, she's happy to be taking pictures for a real job. Plus, she's a materialistic hippie, so the money suits her," she told her friend. "And I haven't been spending *that* much time with her. Mostly, I've been with Preston."

Renée perked up. "The creeper who showed up after studio hours?"

Trihn shook her head. *Leave it to Renée to only remember that part about him.* "He's not a creeper!"

"Oh, no."

"What?"

"You like him!"

"Of course I like him! I'm sleeping with him," she admitted hastily.

Renée's eyes widened. "I thought you weren't going to do that again right away."

"Well, I didn't plan on it." Her cheeks heated, and she lowered her voice. "I mean, I *really* didn't plan it."

"What didn't you plan?" Renée asked, her voice wary.

"Having sex with him backstage at The Met after a performance of *Giselle* last week," she whispered.

"What?" she cried.

"Yeah."

"Were you at least safe?"

Trihn cringed.

Renée's eyes went as big as saucers. "Are you insane? Are you trying to get pregnant?"

"No! I'm on the pill, of course."

"Yeah, but—"

"It just happened. We've been dating for a couple of weeks, and things just…got out of hand."

"You need to be careful, T."

She nodded. "I guess. I don't feel like I need to be careful with him though. I feel like I just want to get swept away and give him my heart and body and—"

Renée held her hand up. "Okay, I get it."

"I've never felt like this before. Fuck, I mean, I had sex with him backstage! That's just…so not me."

"No, it's not."

"Don't use that tone with me." Trihn crossed her arms and leaned back in the booth. "All my life, everyone has told me to be less serious, to cut loose, to *date*. Now that I am, I'm getting flak?"

"Okay, okay. I'm sorry. I didn't mean to mother you. Sometimes, I can't leave that shit at home and be happy. And I will be happy for you, as long as you're not pregnant."

Trihn threw her head into her hands on the table. "I am not pregnant!"

Renée laughed really hard. "I was kidding! Now, what is Mr. Wonderful doing tonight? I have a little time before I have to be home. I wouldn't mind meeting him."

"He's at work," Trihn said with a smile. "But maybe we could stop by his office and bring him coffee or something after dinner."

"Sounds like a plan."

Trihn pulled out her phone and sent Preston a quick text.

I know you're busy at work tonight, but I thought I could bring you coffee. Let me know when you'll have a break.

Trihn and Renée finished up their dinner, and Trihn picked up the tab. She ignored the angry look Renée was shooting her way. She knew that Renée didn't have that much money, and her mom worked too much to try to provide for her kids. Trihn could afford to pick up a meal here and there.

"You didn't have to do that," Renée said as they exited the diner, the bell over the door jingling noisily.

"I know, but I wanted to."

Renée shrugged it off. "Any word from Preston?"

Trihn checked her phone and shook her head. "I guess he's swamped. This will have to be a quick trip."

They took the subway to *Glitz* magazine headquarters.

They ordered coffees downstairs at the Starbucks in the building and then carried them up the elevator to the marketing floor.

Trihn walked right up to the receptionist at the desk. "Hello, excuse me. I was just bringing this for Preston Whitehall."

The pretty brunette behind the desk looked up at her with wide eyes. "Hi! Sorry, but Preston isn't in." She eyed the coffee covetously.

"He's not in?" Trihn asked in disbelief. "He said he was supposed to be here today."

The girl shrugged. "He was earlier. I don't really keep track of everyone's whereabouts. Did you want to wait or something?"

Trihn looked to Renée for support.

She shrugged her shoulders. "Don't know what to tell you. Want to text him again?"

Trihn retrieved her phone and frowned when she didn't see a text message from him. That was so weird. He was always so quick to respond, almost instantaneous normally. *If he isn't working, then what is he doing?*

"He hasn't responded to this one," she murmured.

"Just try one more time."

> *I'm at your work, and the receptionist said that you're not here. What's up?*

They waited for a few minutes to see if he would respond, and then when he didn't, Trihn handed over the extra coffee to the overworked receptionist, thanked her, and left.

"Hey, no big deal!" Renée said, patting her on the back. "I'll meet him another time."

"Yeah."

"Don't let this get you down. You were just raving about him!"

"I know, but…"

"Yes?"

Trihn sighed. "I don't want to think too much into it, but isn't it weird that he told me he'd be at work today, and he's not here?"

"Yeah, a little," she conceded. "But you don't know what he's doing. He could be out on an errand or helping someone with work or doing anything. It's probably best not to freak before you talk to him."

"You're right. I'll just wait to hear from him," Trihn said. Then, she checked her phone. Nothing. "Well, whatever. Forget Preston. I have a little more time to kill. Let's get some fucking doughnuts! It'll probably be the last time I can binge-eat with you before you go to Juilliard." Trihn laughed. "How are you going to live without the occasional street truck doughnut run?"

"I really have no idea."

The girls talked and reminisced about old times while finding a street vendor to fill their craving.

Trihn kept waiting for her phone to buzz in her hand, but it never did—not the whole time she was with Renée, not on the subway ride home, and not when she finally fell into a restless slumber back in Brooklyn.

NINE

Hey, babe. Sorry. Ended up working from home last night, and fell asleep at my computer.

TRIHN STARED DOWN AT THE MESSAGE on her phone. She was glad to have an explanation, but it left her unsettled. She had gotten so worked up about him not responding to her all night. She had actually wanted to take the subway back into the city and go to his apartment for an explanation.

It was inherently irrational. She was *not* that kind of girl—or at least she didn't think she was. She didn't want to turn into a psycho, wondering what he was doing at night when she wasn't there.

There was no reason for her to freak out over a missed phone call.

> *Not a problem. I knew you were busy. Do I get to see you later?*

> *Lunch?*

She agreed to meet up with him at his apartment before he went into work. She was prepared to put the entire thing behind her and just enjoy the time she would have with him.

Half an hour later, she was out the door and on the subway into Manhattan. She texted Renée, promising that she would come in to help with Intensive again after lunch today.

Reaching her stop near Preston's building at NYU, she exited onto a busy street milling with summer students. As she approached her destination, her feet slowed to a stop. Preston was standing at the front entrance to his apartment, talking to a leggy blonde in too-short shorts.

Trihn watched their interaction from a distance. The girl had her hand high against the edifice and was leaning against it. She started laughing and placed her other hand on Preston's arm. Preston cracked up, too. He rested his hip against the wall and tilted his head toward her. He was clearly listening *very* intently to what she had to say.

Trihn took a deep breath. *This is not what it looks like.* She was still jittery from last night, and now, she was seeing things that weren't there.

She walked right up to where Preston was and smiled. "There you are."

The girl didn't even back up or stop smiling at Preston, who had taken a slight step back when he saw Trihn.

"Hey, Trihn," he said casually.

"All ready for our lunch date?" *God, I sound petty.* She hated how her voice had strained over the words.

Whoever this girl was, she had a certain charm. She was shorter with a fuller chest and ass. Trihn's tall, thin body type would never allow her to look like that. Her body was great for ballet, but sometimes, she wished she could fill out her frame.

"Yep. Sounds good. This is my friend Stephanie. We had accounting together last semester," Preston told her.

"Hi," Stephanie said, extending her hand. She looked Trihn over indifferently before turning her gaze back to Preston.

"Hi." Trihn ruefully shook her hand and then pulled it back. "You ready?"

Preston nodded. "See you around, Steph."

"Bye, Preston. I'll catch you around."

As they walked down the street to get lunch, Trihn held her confusion in as best as she could. Clearly, she wasn't doing that great of a job because Preston kept giving her questioning looks. He held the door open for her, and they sat down at a table for two.

"What's on your mind?" he asked.

"Nothing," she said into her menu.

"Trihn"—he reached for her hand and started stroking circles into her palm—"you seem stressed. Is this about me missing your call?"

She sighed heavily. "No. I kind of freaked about that for no reason. I should have guessed you had just gone home early."

"Yeah. I'm working on a big project right now," he explained. "I have so much to do."

"And that's important. I just…I've never really dated like this before," she admitted. She chewed on her bottom lip, mustering up the courage to say what else was bothering her. "You're just friends with that Stephanie girl, right? I don't even know why I would think you were more than friends. I only saw you guys together for all of two minutes, but…" She trailed off, realizing that she was rambling.

Preston laughed and brought her hand to his lips. "Why would you think we were more than friends? You know I'm with you."

"I know. You're right. I just…" She took a deep breath. "I really like you."

"I really like you, too," he said.

"I know I shouldn't worry, but it's kind of part of my personality. I always struggled with worrying in modeling and ballet. So…I guess I just want to make sure we're on the same page"—she looked up at him with earnest—"that we're moving in the same direction."

"This is all kind of coming out of left field. You shouldn't stress so much. This is fun. I like being with you. We're going to have a great rest of the summer, and then you'll be at NYU next semester. Here, with me."

She nodded. *God, why am I such a stress ball?* She shouldn't be accusing Preston of things when he had done nothing wrong. This relationship was what she wanted, and next semester, she wouldn't have to hop on the subway to see him.

"I'll try not to stress anymore. I wish I could shut my brain down sometimes." She laughed lightly. "I'm just glad we're here together."

He kissed her hand again. "Me, too."

The waiter came over to take their order, breaking the moment between them. She ordered a salad, and he got a burger with fries.

As the waiter walked away, Preston turned his attention back to Trihn. "I do feel bad that you were worried about me last night. I guess I'm just exhausted from this new project. I feel like I'm doing most of the muscle behind the work."

"Isn't that normal for an entry-level position?" she asked even though she knew the answer.

"Yeah. I guess it is, but it was never like this before. We're about to put out a new issue, and we're closing out this huge deal with a diamond company in our advertising space. I feel like I'm doing a million things at once."

Trihn smiled and tried to hide it behind her hand. Only this morning, she had heard about the diamond deal from her mom. She had been listening with half an ear, but it was interesting to have the crossover.

"I get it," she said after a minute. "More than you know."

"What do you mean?"

"Well…" She bit her lip. She hadn't meant to keep this detail from him the first time he told her that he worked for *Glitz*, but then there never seemed to be a good time to mention it. "My mom works for *Glitz*."

"Your mom?"

"Yeah. Linh Hamilton. She's an executive vice president for the company," Trihn admitted.

"Linh…Hamilton," he said the name almost reverently.

"Yeah."

"Hamilton," he repeated.

Trihn started laughing. "Yes! That's my mom. I don't know why I didn't mention it before."

"Me either."

She shrugged. "I guess it slipped my mind. Either way, I get the work thing. I know how much time you have to put in. I decided to help out Renée with this dance Intensive we do every summer for scholarship students anyway, so I'll be busy again."

The conversation veered off course from there as she started telling Preston all the crazy stories and adventures she and Renée had gotten into. He seemed to be lost in thought, but she assumed it was because of his big project at work. She hoped that he would finish it up soon, so they could spend more time together.

Once they were finished, Preston left money to cover the check, and they exited together.

"All right. I have to get to the magazine for a few hours, but can I see you later this week?" he asked.

She smiled and nodded in agreement. "I'd like that," she said, sliding into his embrace. "Actually, I have something to do on Thursday night that you might like."

"Another model party?"

She shook her head. "Better."

He inquisitively arched an eyebrow. "You always leave me guessing."

"Don't act like you don't like it."

"Oh, I do. I'll be there."

TEN

TRIHN COULDN'T BELIEVE SHE WAS DOING THIS.

Just walking up the stairs to Preston's apartment made her jittery. She had already made up her mind. She was going to take Preston with her to Slipper tonight, but that didn't mean that she was any less nervous about it.

No one knew about this place—not Lydia, not Renée, and definitely not her parents. And she was giving this to him.

A part of her couldn't believe that she was going to show him something she had never shown anyone else.

The suspicions she'd had about Preston earlier that week seemed like a distant memory, and at this point, she couldn't deny what she felt for him, how strongly her feelings were. And by bringing him with her today, it would be like they were taking another step forward, crossing an invisible line.

With a deep calming breath, she knocked on the door to his apartment. Heavy footfalls sounded on the hardwood floor on the other side of the door, and then it opened to reveal Preston's smiling face.

"Wow," he breathed when he caught sight of her. He drank her in. His eyes swept down her body, looking over the carefully chosen outfit she had decided on—a jeweled lace bra under a nearly sheer black shirt and tight black shorts paired with her favorite heeled booties.

"You look…" And he just stared.

Trihn laughed. "Thanks. I think."

"You think?" he asked. He took two steps forward, closing the distance between them. His hands moved up and down her sides. "I think we should skip wherever we're going tonight."

"What?"

"No need to go out. Everything I want to do tonight is already here," he said meaningfully.

His blue eyes seared into her, making her forget all about their plans, all about where she was going to take him.

"As much as I'd love to stay in…"

Preston pulled her flush against him and dragged her into the apartment. She couldn't even protest as his lips landed on hers, hot and heavy and full of a thousand promises. Her eyes fluttered closed as she succumbed to the heat traveling through her body. She grabbed the front of his button-up and bunched the material in her hands. She wanted nothing more than to rip his shirt off his body.

He toed the door closed behind them and her eyes popped open. His hands were already underneath her shirt, running over her stomach and up to her bra. She ground her body against him. She could feel him growing harder. Her own body was pulsing in time to each demanding kiss.

Preston was aggressive and on fire tonight. A blush bloomed on her skin, and when he pushed her against the door, her mind returned to that night backstage, causing her lower body to throb at the memory, at what he could be doing to her right now.

"We're going to be late," she breathed as he laid kisses down her neck and rocked his dick against her.

"Then, we'll be quick," he growled.

His hands grabbed her ass, hoisting her legs up and around his waist.

"Oh God," she cried. She could feel him very easily through her shorts.

He lifted her effortlessly and carried her to the wooden dining table. He didn't even bother with walking all the way to the bedroom. His eyes showed that he couldn't wait. Clearing some of the papers off the table, he laid her backward and then unceremoniously wrenched her shorts down to her feet.

He undid the button and zipper on his jeans with a flick of his fingers. His pants dropped to the floor. His hand went into his boxers, and he pulled his dick free. She groaned at the sight of him. Her lower half was already wet when he pressed against her opening. Throwing her head back, she bit her lip at how amazing he felt.

"Mmm," he groaned. "I want to take my time with you."

He pushed in an inch deeper. She moaned and clenched her hands into fists.

"D-don't," she pleaded.

"Don't take my time?" he asked, teasingly sliding the tip in and out of her.

"Please no."

"You want me to fuck you?"

She begged him to do with her eyes.

"We don't have a lot of time. You're going to have to tell me what you want." His eyes were mischievous in the dim lighting.

"Oh God," she said. Embarrassment flushed her skin, but she wasn't about to deny him anything, not with where he was standing at the moment and how desperately she wanted him. "Fuck me, Preston."

He didn't need to be told twice. He shoved all the way inside her without complaint, filling her to the hilt. She closed her eyes and moaned at the feel of him, not having enough cognizant thought at the time to wonder if anyone could hear her.

Preston pressed her legs farther apart and grabbed her hips for leverage. Then, without warning, he started pounding into her. There was nothing gentle in his touch, nothing tender in the way he slid in and out of her. This was nothing but straight violent fucking, and she was enjoying every minute of it.

She felt some pain, but it was so overwhelmed by the intense pleasure rocketing through her that she forgot all else.

Somehow, he picked up his pace. His thrusts were sharp and measured, driving her into a heated frenzy. He said it would have to be quick, and the way he was working her was clearly doing the job. She could already feel the friction pushing her to a climax.

Then, he moved one of his hands to her clit and started rubbing her in demanding slow circles. Her eyes flew back open, and she cried out. It was so much, almost too much. She couldn't think. She could hardly breathe. Everything silenced all around her. She was going to come undone at any minute.

Preston grunted and slammed into her harder. "Come for me, Trihn. I'm so close."

She shuddered, feeling her body release at his command. She had been so worked up and ready to go that the feel of him coming had sent her straight over the edge and into oblivion.

Her breaths came out in uneven spurts as she finally relaxed back against the table.

"Fuck," he murmured.

"What you said."

"Fuck," he repeated.

She laughed. "We're definitely going to be late."

"So worth it."

"Mmhmm," she agreed.

They cleaned up and righted their mussed clothing as best as they could before exiting the apartment. Preston flagged down a cab, and Trihn gave the cabbie the address to Slipper. Fifteen minutes later, they were dropped off on the sidewalk outside the club.

While Preston paid, Trihn tried to get herself together again. She was now bubbling with energy after what had just happened. She didn't care that they were late for the show. She found it hard to care about anything right now.

"Where have you taken me?" Preston asked.

He nuzzled her neck, and she giggled.

"Come on. I'll show you," she said.

She took his hand and walked him down the stairs, passing the sign with a shiny glass slipper on it. The girl at the door was dressed in a tiny dress that sparkled with thousands of tiny sequins. Her hair was pulled up into a blunt bob wig, and she had the most dramatic makeup on her face.

"There you are!" she said, fluttering her two-inch fake eyelashes at Trihn. "We thought you might have bailed on us." Her eyes turned to Preston, and she licked her lips. "I wouldn't have blamed you."

Trihn chuckled. "Just running behind. How much did we miss?"

"Just the opening act. Just wait another minute, and I'll get you two into seats...unless you want to share mine," the girl purred.

She leaned toward Preston, and he shifted an inch closer to Trihn. He raised an eyebrow at her, and she had to cover her mouth to keep from laughing out loud.

"I think we're okay. Thank you," Trihn said.

They heard applause from the other side of the door, and the woman opened it for them. Once they stepped inside, they were transported into another world, a fairy tale. The club had taken over the two floors above it and created a large open room with a giant floor-level stage in the middle. Plush couches fit for royalty circled the stage. People dressed in mock court attire circulated the room, taking orders and offering drinks. It was magical.

"Right this way."

Trihn and Preston followed the woman to an empty couch one row back from the stage. A man in a jester costume approached, and Preston ordered drinks for the both of them. He slid his arm around her shoulders, drawing her in closer.

"You brought me *here* when we could have stayed at home?" he asked. Confusion was evident in his voice.

"Just watch," she said. She had to agree that, in that moment, she would much rather be at home, laid out on his dining room table. But she also wanted to share this with him…even if it seemed kind of meaningless now that they were there.

The lights dimmed, and a spotlight shone on a single woman in a white dress in the center of the room.

When she began to move, Preston's eyes widened. "Wha—"

The music was soft and sensual but endearing, and it picked up speed with the girl's fluid movements. Two other girls appeared, as if from thin air, mirroring the dance on the stage. They danced together and apart. Their bodies slid against each other, morphing into one, and then pulled back to reveal two men in their midst. They had the first girl between them, lifting her into the air. She did an aerial flip onto the ground, and the men joined in on the dance.

A cube trapeze contraption descended from the ceiling in the middle of the performance, and the two men lifted the girl again, tossing her into a flip before she caught the bar.

"This is…not ballet," Preston breathed into her ear.

"No, it's not."

They watched, mesmerized, as the two guys performed acrobatic flips with the girl on the square a dozen feet above the ground. It was terrifying and beautiful and erotic.

When they finished, the crowd applauded the dance and feats of athleticism.

Preston turned to her and cocked his head to the side. "I feel like I'm at Cirque du Soleil."

"Well, some of these people used to work for them," she confessed. "Usually, it's just a burlesque club. The acrobatic dance, trapeze, aerials, pole—"

"Pole?" he asked with raised eyebrows and a dirty smirk.

"Not stripping," she insisted. "Just acrobatic pole dancing."

"There's a difference?"

"Trust me. It's much more difficult with many more bruises, and it's not half as sexy as you might think it is. Plus, they keep their clothes on, and they even go to competitions, just like dance or cheer or gymnastics or anything else."

He held his hands up. "I see you're passionate about this. Forgive my ignorance," he said with that same dirty smirk, like he wanted to take her right there on the couch the more vehement she'd become.

"I forgive you," she joked. "But really…I've never brought anyone here before."

"How did you even find this place?"

Trihn shrugged. "My friend Cassidy started performing here after leaving the company at NYC Dance House. She's performing tonight."

"So, do your other friends from the company come here, too?"

Trihn shook her head. "Nah. Cassidy kind of…rubs people the wrong way. She's very…spirited," she mused. "This is my secret. No one else knows about it. So, now, I guess…it's our secret."

"I like secrets."

"Good, because my family would probably kill me if they found out I hung out at places like this."

He laughed and turned back to the stage as the next performers started their routine, and they watched for another hour and a half. As a regular of Slipper, Trihn had seen some of the amazing performances before, but some were brand-new for the show tonight. Every single one of them had given her a rush and reminded her all over again why she loved this so much. It was different than ballet, which was so structured. This was utterly freeing.

Then, Cassidy stepped onto the stage. She was about Trihn's height with a fire-engine red pixie cut and a toned lean body that was accentuated in the tiny silver crop and shorts combo she was wearing.

A long silver pole, reaching up to the ceiling, materialized in the center of the stage. Her movements were unlike anything anyone could have envisioned. The pole was an extension of her body. Watching her move was like a living art piece.

Anyone who believed that pole dancing was only for strippers had never witnessed Cassidy perform. Just because poles were in strip clubs didn't mean that the art form belonged to them. Most strippers couldn't even do the incredible aerial stunts that Cassidy pulled off, thanks to years of training and her incredible gymnastics and dance background. She had come in third this past year at the National Pole Championship in Los Angeles.

Trihn would kill to be in her shoes—to be so sure of her life after high school, so set on her path, so free to do whatever the fuck she wanted.

"She's really good," Preston admitted.

"I know."

"She could be making so much money."

Trihn laughed and nudged him. "She is. Just look at her."

Really, no one could tear their eyes off of the stage when Cassidy performed.

Cassidy climbed the pole higher and higher until she could almost touch the ceiling. The music hit a crescendo, and then in her final move, she dropped straight to the ground, a full thirty-feet free-fall, before tightening her body all around the pole and saving herself from certain death, landing a hairbreadth from the ground.

The crowd gasped and then cheered in an uproar. She was brilliant.

Trihn leaped to her feet, applauding her friend. Preston stood next to her, also mesmerized.

Then, Trihn felt Cassidy's eyes on her. She smiled broad and then rushed from the stage, heading straight to Trihn.

Cassidy latched on to Trihn's wrist. "Come on."

"Cassidy, what are you doing?" Trihn demanded in a panic.

"Your turn, little ballerina."

"What? No!"

"Ladies and gentlemen"—Cassidy's voice boomed through the room—"I would like to present our newest member of the Slipper company, Trihnity," she cheered, pulling a dumbstruck Trihn onto the stage.

ELEVEN

THE CROWD WENT WILD.

Trihn's mouth dropped open. She was standing on the stage at Slipper in front of more than a hundred people and her boyfriend. Cassidy was speaking, but Trihn felt as if she were in a vacuum. She couldn't hear a word of it. All she could do was stand there in shock and wonder what the hell was going on.

Cassidy and some of the other members of Slipper had worked with Trihn backstage and at clubs, teaching her the ropes. She knew enough about pole dancing to perform, but she had never in a million years thought she would actually do it. It was a skill set she'd closely guarded…and had never intended on showing Preston, let alone a roomful of strangers.

Then, Cassidy took a step back with her hand out.

Trihn met her wicked gaze and mouthed, *I'm going to kill you.*

Cassidy cackled. But there was nothing Trihn could do. She had to either perform or slink away and lose face in front of everyone. There wasn't really a choice.

With a heavy sigh, she squared her shoulders and made up her mind. She reached down for her booties, unzipped them, and started taking her shoes off. Her feet sank into the soft spring floor just as the music started. She would have laughed if she wasn't so nervous. She had danced to this song before when they were messing around. Cassidy must have planned this ever since Trihn had told her that she was coming tonight. *That girl will pay for it later.*

The crowd cheered as her shoes were discarded, and Trihn slowly stripped out of her shirt. It was probably completely see-through anyway, thanks to the harsh lighting on the stage, but she would need all the skin she could use to stick to the pole. Thank God she had chosen one of her best bras for the evening.

She could feel Preston's eyes on her, and for a second, she let herself find him in the crowd. He was intrigued, leaning forward in his seat—no, not just intrigued. He was fascinated and desirous.

With the power of that look, she let expectations wash off of her, and a haughty smirk touched her lips. She could do this. She wasn't as good as Cassidy, but that didn't matter. The crowd wanted a show, and a show she would provide.

Trihn slowly reached up and slid her fingers around the pole. It was cool to the touch. She'd thought her hands might be slick, impairing her grip, but she found that she must not be as nervous as she'd thought. She started walking in a slow, sensual circle around the pole, warming her body up as much as drawing the eyes of the crowd.

She picked up the pace until she was nearly running. Then, she dropped her left hand lower on the pole, mirroring her top arm, and kicked her legs up, swinging around the pole with her legs bent at the knees. She pretended to walk through thin air, all while her arms held her up in place, and the crowd cheered.

Her smile grew.

Turning in midair, she brought her low arm up to meet her high arm and used her upper-body strength to pull herself upside down through a shoulder mount before executing a perfect Gemini. With one leg extended and the other wrapped around the pole for support, her body tipped backward, and she stared out at the crowd, completely upside down.

She felt the fluidity of the dance coursing through her. She knew the moves, and she knew how to complete them. Performing came second nature to her.

Soon, she was flying through the moves. Thanks to practices with Cassidy, Trihn had actually felt prepared for this even though she had never performed on the pole before.

Her muscles started aching halfway through the song. She definitely hadn't warmed up, and it had been a while since she danced pole. Luckily, the Intensive practices had kept her ballet body in shape, so she could push herself.

She couldn't end on anything as dramatic as Cassidy's ending, but Trihn forced herself into a split on the bar, grabbed the pole with both hands, and then straightened her elbows out. This released her body from the pole so that the only things keeping her upright and perpendicular to the pole was her flexed foot and both hands. She hadn't done this one in a while, and she pulled herself back to the pole before she could fall on her face. She flipped back onto the stage floor and bowed to applause like she had never heard. People didn't cheer this loud for ballet, even at Dance House showcases.

Cassidy ran back out, grabbed Trihn's arm, and held it high in the air. Trihn couldn't hear what she was saying over the roar of the crowd, and anyway, her eyes were locked on Preston. He wasn't just beaming with excitement. He looked ready to eat her alive.

Cassidy pulled her into a hug. "Don't hate me! You did awesome, chick. You killed that Russian down split."

Trihn gave her a shaky smile. "Thanks, you bitch."

Cassidy laughed and squeezed her tighter.

Trihn picked up her discarded clothing and stumbled back to her seat.

Preston pulled her against him in a fierce hug. "You never told me you could do that!" he cried.

"I've never done that before," she said. All the nerves seemed to hit her at once, and her body was shaking. She felt powerful from her performance, yet her stomach plummeted to the floor as fear set in about what had happened.

"You're trembling."

She laughed. "I know. I can't stop."

"Let's get you out of here."

Preston put his arm around her shoulders and directed her through the crowd just as the last act of the night came onto the stage. Trihn glanced over her shoulder once to take in Slipper just the way it was after her first performance. Then, they disappeared up the stairs and walked out onto the city block.

Cassidy rounded the corner a second later. "Hey, Trihn! I didn't mean to scare you off."

Trihn smiled, letting her nerves settle. "I can't believe you surprised me like that."

"I knew you'd never do it otherwise."

"You're right. I wouldn't have."

"But wasn't it fun?" Cassidy asked with a big smile. "You could work here with me while you go to NYU. Big boss man said he liked your show, and with some work, we could even be a double act!"

Trihn's head swam. "What?" she sputtered.

"That's a great opportunity," Preston said.

She turned to him in a daze, forgetting that he had been there through it all. "It is," she said dumbly.

"Who is this?" Cassidy said, openly eyeing him with a big smile. Cassidy had a tendency to flirt with anyone—even Trihn on occasion.

"This is my boyfriend, Preston," Trihn said. It was the first time she had ever claimed him as such, and it felt good.

"Oh! Nice! Good choice," Cassidy purred. "Well, think on it. Don't tell me tonight. You're still drunk on a performer's high to decide now."

"I'll think on it," she told her friend.

Cassidy kissed Trihn on the cheek and then fluttered her fingers at Preston with a pointed wink before walking to the backstage door.

"You know," Preston said with a laugh, "she kind of seems into you."

"What?" she asked in surprise. "No way. Cassidy is just into everyone."

"Well, definitely you."

"No way," she repeated.

He raised his eyebrows. "I'm just saying, she might be interested in joining us."

It was Trihn's turn for her eyebrows to rise. "Like...*with* us?"

Preston shrugged. "I'm not saying I want to share you, but you two would make a pretty great double act," he said, mirroring Cassidy's language.

"For a dance performance!" Trihn said, out of her element. "Would you...be into *that*?"

Preston pulled her tighter to him and kissed her on the mouth. "I'm into whatever you're into. Can't blame a guy for trying."

She laughed against his mouth and shook her head. No, she supposed she couldn't blame him for trying. Cassidy was beautiful, and all guys were into threesomes...even if Preston was trying to brush it aside like he didn't care.

A cab drove by in that moment, and Preston put his hand out to flag it down. Their conversation was forgotten as they drove back across town.

Preston couldn't keep his hands to himself in the car. "What you did up there," he breathed into her ear in the backseat, "I've never seen anything like it." His hands traveled up her bare thighs. "Earlier, you said that it's not sexy, but you're dead wrong. It's sexy as hell."

He fluttered his fingers against her inner thighs. It took her strength of will to keep from moaning against him and opening her legs.

"It got me hard as a rock. I wanted nothing more than to drag you out right then and there."

"Preston," she hissed. She didn't think that the driver could hear him, but it didn't help with her growing desire.

"All I could think about was fucking you on my dining room table and everything I was going to do to you when I got you home."

She bit her lip and turned to look up into his blue eyes. "You're killing me."

"Don't worry." He nipped on her bottom lip and flicked his tongue against the sensitive skin. "I'm never letting you out of my apartment after that show."

And he made that perfectly clear throughout the rest of the night.

TWELVE

Trihnity Camila Hamilton! Answer your phone right now, or you will find yourself without one!

THROUGH BLEARY EYES, Trihn stared down at the message from her mother. *Shit!*

She sat up in Preston's bed and stretched her sore muscles. Literally everything hurt. Whether from her pole performance or from the marathon sexcapades last night, she didn't know. She cracked her neck, fingers, spine, and hips as she stood, and then she groaned.

"This is a welcome sight this early in the morning," Preston said, eyeing her naked body.

"I can't move."

k.a. linde

He reached for her. "Then, I guess you can't leave."

"I'm not sure it's physically possible for me to have sex with you again," she said with a chuckle as she searched around the room for her discarded clothing.

"I can change your mind." He came up behind her and pressed his bare chest against her back. He started kissing down her neck.

For a split second, she let herself get lost in his kisses. He was so good at that. Her aches and pains disappeared under his lips.

Then, she remembered the text message on her phone and sighed.

"Sorry. My mom is freaking. I have to go." She turned around and slid her arms around his neck. "I can't wait until school starts, and then I won't have to leave for anything in the morning, except school."

He kissed her, deeply and hungrily, and she thought that she might give in all over again, but then his phone started ringing. He groaned and then jogged over to the other side of the room. He picked up the phone from the nightstand and silenced it.

"Fuck," he groaned.

His eyes darted between Trihn and his phone.

"You can get it," she said, finding her bra on the arm of his chair. *How did it get there?* "I'm just heading out."

"No, it can wait." He checked the face of the phone again and then set it aside, facedown. "I'm just going to hop into the shower."

"All right. I'll talk to you later?"

"Of course." He walked back over and kissed her just as his phone started ringing again.

96

Trihn laughed. "Someone clearly wants to talk to you."

"It's not important."

"Well, I have to go anyway," Trihn said between kisses.

"When can I see you again?"

"Tonight?" she asked.

She tried to extricate herself from his arms, but he kept pulling her closer.

"I have to work tonight."

"Tomorrow night?"

"What about tomorrow before I go to work?"

He smirked down at her, and she couldn't help from laughing.

"I'll see if I can get away."

Trihn kissed him one last time and then dashed out of the apartment just as his phone rang for the third time that morning. She shook her head. Whoever was calling seriously needed to get ahold of him.

She hurried out of his building and onto the subway. She sent a text to her mom, letting her know that she was on her way home, and she was shocked to get a reply that her mother was still at home, waiting for her.

"Great," she grumbled.

When the subway deposited her back in Brooklyn, Trihn trudged the block from the stop to her parents' house. She was not looking forward to this conversation. Her parents were pretty chill about most things other parents might freak out about, but her mom must be pissed if she had stayed home from work to wait for Trihn.

She entered the house, fully aware that she was still dressed in the clothes that she had left the house in yesterday.

She was halfway to the stairs when her mother called out to her, "Trihn, is that you?"

She sighed heavily. "Yep. It's me, Mom."

"Come into the kitchen, so we can talk."

Trihn took a deep breath and then walked into the kitchen. "What's up?"

Her mother looked her up and down with no more than a raised eyebrow. "If you're going to stay out all night, you should at least let me know. And don't tell me that you were with Lydia this time because she didn't know where you were either."

"I wasn't with Lydia," Trihn said.

"Clearly. You were with a boy, I'm sure."

Trihn shrugged. "I'm going to be in college in a month. What does it even matter who I'm with or where I am at night?"

"Because you're not in college yet!" Linh snapped. She sighed and pinched the bridge of her nose. "And I miss you."

"Okay," Trihn said quickly. She hadn't meant to upset her mom. She hadn't really thought of anything last night when she stayed the night at Preston's apartment. It had just felt right at the time. "I'll let you know where I am next time."

"Thank you," Linh said. "I wasn't trying to argue with you. I was worried."

"You don't have to worry about me, Mom."

"You're my daughter. It comes with the territory."

Trihn walked forward and enveloped her mom in a hug. She smiled and kissed the top of her mother's head.

"I'm just going to take a quick shower and change," Trihn told her.

She was happy that her mother wasn't actually that angry with her. It was just the case of the youngest moving out of the house.

"Wait one minute," Linh said, calling Trihn back to her side.

"Yeah?"

"You know I'm happy for you…that you've found someone."

Trihn nodded.

"And I just thought I would offer, since Lydia is bringing her boyfriend on our annual summer vacation, that you could bring yours. I wouldn't mind meeting this man who has stolen my daughter's heart," Linh said.

Trihn wrinkled her nose. She wasn't the type to invite her boyfriend on a family vacation.

Every year for a week or two before school started, her family would go to the Hamptons and vacation with her mother's colleague Betty and her family. They had a son, Ian, who was Trihn's age, so it was more fun to spend her time hanging out with him than bringing some guy she had just met, like Lydia did every trip.

"Ugh…Lydia is dating someone new?"

Linh shrugged her thin shoulders. "You know your sister. We always accommodate her free spirit."

"Seriously, how many boyfriends has she brought on vacation?"

"I'm certain even she has lost count," Linh said. "Now, are you going to invite your boyfriend, so we can have some balance?"

Trihn cringed. "I don't know, Mom. It's so new…"

"It's up to you, of course, but he is more than welcome."

"All right. Well, I'll ask him, but I can't guarantee anything."

Linh smiled. "I'm sure he'll come around. How could anyone resist my beautiful daughter?"

"Oh, please, Mom." Trihn walked up the stairs and hurried into the shower. She didn't want to think about inviting Preston on vacation with them. *Are we there yet in our relationship?*

After last night, she really thought they were. He saw her, all of her, like no one else ever had, and he had completely accepted her. *Why shouldn't I invite him to go on vacation with me?* That was a completely normal and natural thing to do.

When she got out of the shower, she stared down at her phone, but then she chickened out. She would ask him later. He was at work now. She told herself it had nothing to do with her being scared to ask him. It was only practical to wait until he could check his phone and get back to her.

Trihn changed into dance clothes and tied her hair up into a bun. She was going to meet Renée for Intensive. There were only a few more weeks of it left, and Trihn would be gone for at least one of those. She was just glad she would be back in time to see the final performances of the students she had been working with throughout much of the summer. Then, there would be only two more weeks until school started.

Making her way back into the city, she hurried along to the studio. She was not looking forward to working out her very sore muscles, but the aches reminded her of last night, and she couldn't keep the shit-eating grin off her face.

"What's that for?" Renée asked.

"What?"

"You look like you just got away with murder."

Trihn laughed. "Just happy I guess."

"Preston?"

Trihn nodded. "I'm inviting him to the Hamptons."

"*Oh*. Fancy!" Renée said. "Are you turning into Lydia now?"

"No!" Trihn protested. "Preston and I are actually serious."

Renée shrugged. "Well, has he agreed to go?"

"I haven't asked him yet."

Renée rolled her eyes and reached for Trihn's phone. "Oh my God! Give me the phone, and I'll send the text myself."

"I don't need your help!" Trihn said, pulling her phone back. "I'll send it now."

> *Hey, I'm going on vacation with my parents in two weeks. They offered you an invitation to join us for the week, and I'd love it if you could come with me.*

Trihn pressed Send and fidgeted as she waited for his response. Her phone dinged, and she looked down at it.

"And?" Renée prodded as she read over her shoulder.

> *I'll check with work and get back to you.*

"That's not a very upbeat answer," Renée said.

No, it's not.

"He works a lot. He might not be able to get off."

"Uh-huh."

"Don't *uh-huh* me," Trihn snapped.

"I still think he's a little creepy with the way he stalked you."

"He didn't stalk me! We've been through this."

"Well, whatever. We have a class to teach, so worry about the BF later," Renée teased.

"Fine."

Trihn put her phone away into her dance bag. But just as she was about to walk away to go to the barre, it dinged. She reached for it to check the message, hoping for good news.

> *I just asked my boss. He said the weeks up until I get back into school are the most important. Sounds like a no-go. Sorry, babe.*

Oh…

Disappointment—it was completely stupid to feel it. She hadn't even wanted to invite Preston on vacation. That wasn't *her* at all. Then, she had let hope weasel in, and she had actually considered that it would be a good idea. Even on short notice, she thought it might be possible. Then, her high hopes had deflated just as quickly as they'd come.

"What?" Renée asked, the concern evident in her voice.

Trihn must have really looked like shit to elicit that reaction from her. She normally had a casually playful tone full of sarcastic humor.

"Nothing," Trihn said, quickly stashing her phone

"You can't bullshit me. What did he say?" Renée took two steps toward Trihn and yanked the phone out of her hand. She read the message and then handed it back.

"Yeah, he can't go," Trihn said. She chewed on her lip and glanced away from her friend.

"Hey, if you're not up for Intensive today, then you can head out. I can handle it," she said consolingly.

"No, I'm fine."

"Stop saying that. You're clearly upset."

"Renée, can we not?"

"Preston is your first boyfriend, and you put your heart on the line, inviting him to this. He probably doesn't even know it, but I do."

"Yeah, well, I feel stupid for being upset." Trihn swiped at her eyes. *God, now tears?*

She took a deep breath. She would never have had tears like this if Renée hadn't asked her about it. She could have held it together through dance, and then it all would have just gone away. It was always the worst when someone asked if she was okay. It was as if the minute someone cared, her walls would crumble.

"You're not stupid." Renée slid her arm around Trihn's shoulders. "You're just human. I know you wear your heart on your sleeve, no matter how serious or how much of a tough girl you are."

Trihn shrugged. "Nothing I can do now. Let's just go dance."

She left Renée behind as she strolled to the barre.

Planting her feet in first position and resting her hand featherlight on the barre were the only things that Trihn let occupy her mind. She wasn't going to think about Preston or vacation, which just meant a week without him, or anything else. She was just going to focus on her body lowering into a plié, the feel of her feet rising up onto pointe in a relevé, and the burn in her legs as she pushed her body to the limit.

THIRTEEN

THE SHOWER BEAT DOWN ON TRIHN'S HEAD, blocking out the pulse hammering against her temples. Ballet had temporarily alleviated the pain and disappointment of what had happened before class, but the anger had continued to simmer just under the surface, giving her a headache.

She shut off the shower and threw back two Tylenol she'd retrieved from her dance bag. She took a swig out of her mostly empty water bottle and waited for the miracle to set in.

"T, I'm heading out. Are you ready?" Renée called.

"Yeah, I'm coming." She wound her hair up into a tight ponytail on top of her head and then slid into the clothes she had come in—loose-fit gray shorts, a white V-neck T-shirt, and black-and-silver slipper ballet flats.

With a deep breath, she set out for the exit with Renée. They both jumped when they found a figure standing in the foyer of the dance studio. It was late, way after-hours for anyone but a student to have access to the company.

"Sorry, we're not open," Renée called.

But as they drew closer, Trihn recognized the person in front of her. "It's all right."

They stopped in front of Preston. He had a worry line in between his eyebrows. His perfect lips were pursed with concern. She wanted to reach out and hug him, to try to comfort him for whatever he was feeling, but she didn't move. She still keenly felt the sting of rejection.

"Hey. What are you doing here?" she asked.

"Came to see you."

Trihn crossed her arms over her chest. "I thought you had to work."

Renée coughed next to Trihn and then pushed her own hand out. "I'm Renée, Trihn's friend."

"Hi, Renée." He shook her hand. "Nice to meet you."

"You, too. Take care of my friend," she said with a slight warning in her voice. "I'm just going to head out and leave you two alone." Renée tossed keys on a blue keychain to Trihn. "Lock up after you leave."

"Thanks. I will."

Renée left them in a hurry, clearly feeling the wave of tension between them.

Had it really only been this morning when I woke up in his arms, desperate to never leave?

For some reason, as they stood apart now, it felt like a lifetime ago.

"So, this is your studio?" he asked.

She nodded.

"Can you show me around?" He smiled tentatively. "I want to see where you spend all your time."

"Sure," she whispered.

She didn't exactly want to play like everything was fine. She was upset but not at him. She was more upset with herself for wanting him to go with her so badly when she had never wanted that before. She just didn't know how to channel that anger.

He took her hand, and they walked around the studio through the open foyer, down the hallway where the administrative offices were, past the empty dressing rooms, and around to all the dance studios. She ended the tour in the studio she and Renée had just been working in.

Trihn walked Preston over to the far wall, which had floor-to-ceiling glass windows overlooking the New York City street below. He was so silent, and she wished she knew what he was thinking. She didn't even know what he was doing here.

She couldn't hold in all the emotions swirling through her any longer. "Why are you here?" she blurted.

"Do I need a reason to come see you?"

"You've never visited me at dance before."

"Not true," he said quickly.

"Not since that first night."

"I know, but you sounded upset in your text, and then you never responded to my other messages."

"I was in dance. I didn't check them."

"Or you were avoiding me," he said.

It was a pretty astute assessment. She hadn't wanted to think about anything, so she hadn't checked her phone.

"Not on purpose."

Preston's fingers curled around her elbow, and he pulled her toward him. "You're mad at me."

"I'm not," she insisted.

"You are." His hands circled her waist, and then he planted a kiss on her forehead.

"No, I'm really not." She sighed heavily.

The feel of him against her just strengthened her resolve. She wasn't mad at him. She wanted him too much, in dangerous amounts. And him being here was showing her that clear as day.

"I've just never invited anyone to go with me on vacation before."

He looked down at her with earnest. "You know I would go with you if I could get off work."

"I know," she insisted. "I just think I was so excited for you to come with me before I even asked you. I know we've only known each other for a couple of months, but what we have is so much more than I expected. I never really dated seriously before you. It just never felt right, but it does with you. So, I guess I got my hopes up that you would be able to go with me, and I understand your reasons for not going, but I can't stop myself from feeling this way. Now, I'm babbling..."

Preston leaned down and pressed his lips to hers. She could feel the tension rolling off of her. She stopped thinking and let herself get caught up in his embrace.

"I know, Trihn," he murmured against her lips. "I get it."

"I don't think you do." She firmly pressed her mouth to his once more before confessing the truth that had been resting on her tongue, "I love you."

"I love you," she repeated.

The words had slipped out of her mouth with unstoppable conviction. She had known for weeks but hadn't allowed herself to think the actual words.

This isn't normal, is it? She wasn't supposed to fall in love this quickly. She was strong and independent and didn't need a man. But when she looked up into Preston's bright blue eyes, she knew she was lost. She knew she loved him. There was no going back from this point.

"Trihn—"

"It's okay," she said hastily when she realized he hadn't said anything back. "You don't have to respond. I didn't think you would."

She bit her lip and looked down.

"Trihn—" he repeated.

"I don't want you to feel pressured to reciprocate. We haven't been dating for that long," she said. Her anxiety was peaking. She had just confessed her feelings to the first boy she ever loved, and now, she felt like an idiot.

"Trihn!"

"What?" she asked, finally looking up at him.

"Just shut up."

Preston latched on to the back of her neck and crushed his lips down onto hers. A flush rose to the surface of her skin. Her breathing was labored. Her eyes were pressed firmly closed, and everything else all around her shut down. His lips were a dose of adrenaline to her system, waking her up and fueling her forward.

Her fingers twined into his hair, and she slid her body against his until no room was left between them. His tongue slipped into her mouth and massaged against her own. His mouth was hot and welcoming. Everything in her surrendered to that kiss.

What little resistance she had left crumbled under his skilled lips, the taste of his tongue, and the slight pressure on the small of her back. Want was a live thing inside of her, and Preston fulfilled what she so desperately craved.

His hands ran down her back and hoisted her legs up and around his hips. She gasped against him as he lowered to his knees right there in the ballet studio overlooking the entire city below them. But no one else existed. It was just their two bodies silhouetted against the glass, coming together in an act of love.

Preston lowered her to the black marley floor and immediately covered her body with his own. He pressed his dick against the thin layer of material of her shorts. She groaned and rocked her pelvis up toward him.

His laugh was deep and guttural in her ear.

"What?"

He started kissing his way down her front. "I'm going to take my time with you."

She practically purred at the comment.

He pushed her shirt up her flat stomach and slowly dragged it over her head before tossing it away from them. His lips fluttered around her breast before one of his fingers dipped under her black bra. She arched her body as he flicked his finger against the erect nipple. His other hand reached under her body and eased the hooks out of the eyes. The bra fell away from her and was slung in the same direction as her shirt.

"Fuck me," he groaned before taking a nipple into his mouth and kneading her breast with his hand. "This body."

He moved to the other breast, making sure each had equal amounts of attention, before landing kisses down the curve of her stomach. He swirled his tongue around her belly button and then trailed it to the waistband of her shorts. Hooking his finger under the edge, he lingered against her sensitive skin, teasing her. She bit into her lip to keep from begging.

His eyes were alight and mischievous when he looked back at her. He was completely in control of himself and her body. She wouldn't have changed it for the life of her.

"Guess you don't need these," he teased.

Her shorts and thong disappeared in one swift tug, and before she had a chance to respond, he buried his face between her legs. She couldn't hold in her cries as he ran his tongue along her clit and forced her legs to open farther for him.

He licked, sucked, and nibbled on her until she bucked beneath him. She wasn't sure she was going to be able to handle anything more, and then his fingers found the opening to her lips.

"Mmm," she sighed.

He swirled his fingers through her wetness, coating them, before sliding them inside her pussy.

"I fucking love the feel of you tightening around my fingers like that," he said from between her legs. "Tighter, babe. I want to feel you fuck my fingers like you would my dick."

His words fueled her desire, and she tightened even more without even thinking about it. Her walls squeezed him so hard that she couldn't believe she hadn't already orgasmed.

"Yes"—he flicked his tongue against her clit again—"that's what I want."

"Oh, fuck," she cried out.

"My turn. I'm going to finger-fuck you until you're dripping on this floor, until you come so hard that you see stars," he promised. His fingers started pumping in and out, harder and faster, before they curled up into her, finding the perfect spot to send her over the edge.

She came just as hard as he'd promised. Her lower half exploded all at once, and a muffled cry escaped her lips. Her walls were still clenching around his fingers as she finished.

"Now, I'm going to take what's mine." He slid his fingers out from her still-quivering body and playfully swiped his fingers against her clit.

She yelped and pulled back. She hadn't recovered enough to even be touched there.

He chuckled and immediately started stripping out of his clothes. When he freed himself from his boxers, she had her own smirk at seeing what her orgasm had done to him. He was as hard as a rock and practically throbbing to get inside her.

"Wait," she said, before he positioned himself in front of her.

If he did that, she would never be able to stop him. Her mind would completely shut off, and she owed him more than that.

Trihn came up to her knees and ran her fingers up his thighs before taking his cock in her hands. "I want you to feel this, too."

To feel my love.

She didn't give him a moment to protest, not that she thought he would. She wrapped one hand around the base of his dick and then wet the head, swirling her tongue around in a circle. He steadied himself with a hand in her hair as she took him all the way into her mouth. Then, she started bobbing back and forth, sucking him until she was sure he couldn't grow any bigger.

His moans filled the space, bringing a smile to her face. Then, his fingers tightened in her hair, and he started thrusting into her mouth. She still had control of him, but he didn't seem to be able to stop either. He was so close. She was sure she was going to feel him hitting the back of her throat at any second, but she still didn't stop.

Just when she thought he was going to come undone, he harshly pulled back and stumbled backward a step, away from her.

Her eyes went wide in panic, and she sat back on her heels in confusion. "What?"

He was breathing heavily as he stared down at her. "If I'm coming, I'm coming inside of that pussy."

Her mouth gaped open in surprise at the crude words, but she didn't protest. *Isn't that exactly what I want?*

Preston closed the distance between them and forced her onto her back again. Her heart thudded in her chest as she spread her legs wide for him.

This was it. She was giving herself to him, giving him everything. He'd had her before but not like this, not with the knowledge that she loved him. This time it felt like so much more.

His hands clasped down on her hips and dragged her an inch closer to him before he plunged deep into her. She kept her eyes trained on his beautiful face as he pumped into her over and over again. They were both so worked up from the foreplay that she knew they were going to hold out for long. He had almost come in her mouth. There was no way he could resist it while being inside her.

Trihn ran her hands up his arms and pulled his face back down toward her. She passionately kissed him with all the love in her heart as she gave her heart, body, and soul to him.

And as she came for a second time, she once again whispered the words to him in earnest, "I love you."

FOURTEEN

"I LOVE YOU. I'll always love you," Preston coos into my ear.
I lean back into his arms with a sigh. This is right.

"Honey, did you need to stop?" Linh asked.

Trihn shook herself from her daydream in frustration and stared at her mom sitting in the passenger seat of their Mercedes SUV while her dad drove.

A week had passed since she confessed her love to Preston. He hadn't responded, but she was sure he felt the same. She didn't want to rush him even though she couldn't help but think about it and what it would be like when he said those three beautiful words. Unfortunately, for the next week, she would be on her stupid family vacation without him.

"No, Mom, I don't need a break. We're almost to the Hamptons anyway," she said, slumping back in her seat.

Her mom gave her a motherly look that said she wasn't going to take this attitude from her youngest daughter throughout the entire vacation. Trihn just slid her Bose headphones out from her oversize Kate Spade bag and drowned out all the other noise in the car. She wouldn't mind going back to that daydream.

She checked her phone for the umpteenth time and sighed at the lack of response. She knew Preston was working and not normally all that talkative during the day anyway, but still…she missed him. She hadn't even gotten to say good-bye because he was so busy.

As she and her parents drove into the Hamptons, Trihn's eyes slid over the stunning mansions. Each was bigger and more outdone than the next. For someone who had grown up and lived her entire life in a townhouse surrounded by millions of other people, the giant houses and wide open spaces in the Hamptons were a thankful reprieve from the city. But by the end of the week, she was always ready to get back to her home.

Her father turned down the street where the house they rented for a week every year sat as untouched and as beautiful as ever. She slipped her headphones off her ears and leaned forward in the seat.

"Glad to be back?" her father, Gabriel, asked.

She nodded. "Yeah. A lot of good memories here."

He pulled into the driveway and parked in one of the three empty garages. Trihn popped open her door and hopped out, inhaling the balmy sea air.

"Where's Ly?" Trihn asked. "I thought she came up yesterday."

Linh waved her hand. "Oh, I asked her to pick up some things that I forgot for the welcome party tomorrow night."

"You got her to go to the store for you?" Trihn asked with wide eyes.

"Lydia was happy to help."

Trihn rolled her eyes. That didn't sound like her sister. "Okay," she said disbelievingly.

She grabbed her bag off the floor of the SUV and trudged toward the house. She was halfway up the stairs when her mother called her back into the kitchen.

Trihn sighed and then ditched her bag at the foot of the stairs. "What?"

Linh held up a piece of paper and waved it at her. "Seems Mr. Peterson has already been over, looking for you," she said with a knowing smile.

"It's *just* Ian, Mother, no Mr. Peterson and definitely none of those looks."

"I've no idea what you're talking about."

"Sure," Trihn said with a shake of her head. In the next minute though, she was out of the house and jogging across the immaculate lawn to the house next door.

She knocked and waited for two seconds for someone to answer the door. When no one did, she let herself inside. "Ian!" she called.

Feet pounded the floor upstairs and then came down the giant winding staircase at the front of the house. Ian appeared a second later with a huge grin on his face. "Trihn! You guys made it!"

He jumped the last three steps and pulled her into a giant hug. She wrapped her arms around his neck and squeezed him a little bit tighter. It had been forever since she saw him. Normally, their parents would vacation in Aspen during the winter or some kind of Caribbean vacation destination during the spring, but Trihn had been occupied with modeling during the Aspen trip and his parents had been too busy for an island vacation last spring.

"It's so good to see you," she told him honestly before pulling back.

Ian was like a brother to her. They had known each other practically their whole lives. Having someone always around who was her age had probably been one of the reasons she hadn't cared about bringing a friend along on vacation with her. She always had one. The thought made her feel equal parts sad that Preston couldn't be here and happy that at least she wouldn't be bored.

"It's great to see you, too. Tell me everything I've missed."

He ushered her through the foyer, past the enormous kitchen, and out the back door to a massive deck that looked out across the Olympic-size pool and to the ocean beyond. Papers were laid out on a table, and Ian's MacBook Pro along with an assortment of odds and ends held them down from blowing away in the breeze.

"What are you working on, genius?" she joked, peering down at the screen.

He laughed. "Things your tiny brain could never comprehend."

"Just because my brain doesn't think in zeros and ones does not make it tiny!" she said, swatting at his arm.

"My brain doesn't think in terms of fashion though."

"Clearly."

"Hey, hey!"

"You've been wearing the same outfits since you were knee-high. I mean, did you walk out of Martha's Vineyard or something?"

Ian's ears turned bright pink at her comment, and she couldn't help but laugh. As soon as he sat down, she fell into the seat next to his and kicked her feet up onto his lap. Teasing Ian was practically an art form as far as she was concerned.

"I'm just surprised you're not wearing anything studded today," he observed.

"Are you sure?" she asked with a wink.

Now, his entire face was beet-red.

She cackled at his reaction. "I'm just kidding!"

"I know."

She shook her head. After all this time, he still got so embarrassed around her.

"Are you excited for Columbia?"

"Very. In two weeks, I'll be in the city for good."

Ian's parents had relegated themselves to a suburb when he entered middle school. As much as they'd wanted to send him to a private school in the city, they'd also wanted him to have a *real* childhood, whatever that meant.

To them, it meant, not in the city.

To Trihn, that sounded ridiculous.

Trihn and Ian eased into a conversation like no time had passed at all, and after an hour, she had let her worries from the city slide away. Preston would be there when she got back, and until then, she needed to enjoy her last summer before college started.

"Hello, Trihn, dear," Ian's mother, Betty, said, stepping out onto the deck. She wore a sleek white dress and heels. Her hair was a perfect slicked-back bun, and her makeup was flawless.

"Hello, Mrs. Peterson," Trihn said with a smile.

"Your mother called and asked for you to return home."

Trihn nodded and stood. "I'll check you later, Ian. Want to come over for dinner? Mom actually got Lydia to go to the store, so who knows what it will be? But you know my mom is a fantastic cook."

"Sounds good. I'll see you then."

"Bye, Mrs. Peterson!" she called before traipsing back through the house and out the door.

Trihn jogged across the lawn with a giant smile on her face. Her hair blew out behind her in the breeze, and she took a deep breath. This felt good and right.

When Trihn rounded the corner, she saw Lydia's car parked in the garage. That must be why her mom had wanted Trihn to come home—time to meet the new boyfriend, the new flavor of the week. Trihn really wasn't looking forward to pretending for a person who wouldn't be around long past this vacation, but she would put on a good face for her sister.

As she started toward the house, she noticed a figure walking out of the garage with a plastic bag dangling from his arm.

Trihn froze. She was seeing things, daydreaming all over again.

Then, he took another step forward.

She would recognize that gait anywhere.

Preston.

"Oh my God!" Trihn cried.

Then, she was running. Her feet carried her faster than she had ever known they could, heading straight toward him.

He's here after all! It must have just been an act, one big front, so he could surprise me like this so completely.

She never would have guessed in a million years that he would be able to pull this off, but it had worked. Now, he was here, and they could be together.

"You're here!" she said as she approached him.

"Preston!" Lydia called from the door. "Don't forget to grab the champagne out of the side door. You know how I like my bubbly!"

Trihn skidded to a halt right in front of Preston, her heart hammering in her chest. She looked in disbelief between the open door and Preston's face. *How did Lydia know Preston? And how could he know what kind of drinks she liked?* He had just gotten here to surprise her.

Then, Trihn really looked into those blue eyes, and her stomach dropped out of her body.

"No," she whispered.

Her world disintegrated before her eyes.

He wasn't here for Trihn.

He was here for *her.*

"Coming, babe," Preston called back to Lydia, his face stretching into a slow painful smile.

FIFTEEN

"DID YOU HEAR ME?" LYDIA ASKED.

She leaned her body out the door. Her eyes caught on Preston, and she had the biggest smile Trihn had ever seen on her sister's face. Then, she seemed to notice Trihn standing there.

"Trihn! There you are!" Lydia burst out of the house and rushed to her. "Mom said you were visiting Ian. Sorry, I had her call you back, but I was so excited for you to meet my boyfriend! This is Preston. Preston, this is my little sister, Trihn."

Trihn swallowed the horror on her face. It was hard to reel in, but somehow, she locked away the parts of her that had shattered into a million pieces, so she could face her sister. This wasn't the way that Lydia needed to find out about Preston. Trihn wasn't even sure she would be able to form words to explain what had happened anyway. In fact, she was a little worried about the use of words in general.

"Nice to meet you," Preston said. He extended his hand out to her, as if this were really the first fucking time they were meeting, as if he honestly expected her to fucking touch him after this.

"Is it?" she growled out.

"I've heard so much about you," he retorted, dropping his hand. "It's nice to finally put a face to the name."

"Funny. Lydia hasn't said a word about you."

"Trihn! Geez, calm down."

Trihn was the furthest thing from calm. She was ready to rip his fucking head off. There was no explanation for this. None. Zero. Zip. Zilch. There was only anger and fury and pain. Great lancing pain was slicing through every limb in her body and piercing her with a fiery hot poker.

Lydia reached for Preston and drew him closer to her. "So sorry," Lydia whispered so soft that Trihn almost didn't hear her.

"It's all right," Preston said. He squeezed her hand.

Trihn tightly clenched her jaw and tried to hold back the rage boiling under the surface.

Half of her wanted to lay into him about the bullshit in front of her, and the other half wanted to run as fast and as far as she could to get away from the nightmare before her eyes.

"You're right," Trihn said. "No reason for me to be irritated that you're bringing random guys on vacation with your family. You always bring total strangers with you."

Preston arched his eyebrow in question. But she didn't know what he was asking.

"God! What's with you?" Lydia asked. "She's not normally like this, Preston."

"Yeah, I'm not. This behavior is completely out of character. Normally, I'm all rainbows and sunshine," she said dramatically. She crossed her arms over her chest to close herself off from them.

"I can see that," Preston said with that goddamn chuckle.

He was actually fucking amused by her behavior. She was going to rip him apart.

"Just go inside with that," Lydia told Preston. "I need a minute alone with my sister."

"All right, babe," he said, as if whatever was about to happen between Lydia and Trihn meant nothing to him. As if…he hadn't called Trihn babe before.

Trihn glared at his back as he departed. *How dare he call Lydia babe! How dare he be dating my sister! How dare he stand there as if he didn't give a shit that this was killing me! How dare that motherfucking asshole!*

"What the fuck is wrong with you?" Lydia exploded. She grabbed Trihn's arm and yanked her sister farther away from the door, so she could spout venom without being heard by her precious flavor of the week.

"What's wrong with *me*?" Trihn cried. She wrenched out of her sister's grip. She didn't give a shit who heard them. "What's wrong with you, bringing a guy you just met on our fucking family vacation?"

"You have no idea what you're talking about! Preston and I have been dating all summer!"

"What?" Trihn sputtered, stumbling backward, as if she had been slapped.

"Yeah! We're in the same program at NYU to receive credit for our summer internships. We met *months* ago at the orientation meeting."

All the air whooshed out of Trihn's lungs as realization hit her. This wasn't some fling. This wasn't someone who Lydia had been fooling around with and invited on vacation on a whim. She was actually seriously dating Preston. They had been dating for several months. *Fucking hell!* They had been dating even longer than Trihn had known Preston—a month longer, if memory served, since that was when Lydia had started her photography internship.

"All summer?" Trihn asked, her voice sounding small and distant due to the ringing in her ears.

"Yes," Lydia snapped. "And if you get off your high horse and give him a chance, you might even like him instead of judging me and the guys I bring home!" She shook her head and then started to head back inside.

Trihn didn't *like* Preston. She was madly in love with him. And all of this was so, so wrong.

"Lydia, wait!" Trihn called before Lydia opened the door.

"What?" Lydia asked. Her anger dissipated as quickly as it had come. It always did with Lydia. She always won, and her life was perfect. *What reason would she have for holding on to anger?*

"I don't think this is such a good idea," Trihn said. She tried to find the words to warn her sister without coming right out and saying it. "What do you even know about this guy?"

Lydia sighed heavily, pushing forward into the house again without an answer.

Trihn anxiously followed behind her. "Lydia, I'm serious!"

"Look, just because *your* boyfriend couldn't come with you doesn't mean you can question mine. You guys have only been dating for a short while, too, right?" Lydia asked.

Lydia's words carried down the hall, and their mother stuck her head through the doorway. "Is everything all right, girls?"

Trihn looked up to see her mother, her father, and Preston staring at them. She gritted her teeth but didn't look away. She was ready to explode at any second.

"Yes, we're fine," Lydia said. She bounced from one foot to the other with a giant grin. "I was just asking about Trihn's boyfriend."

Preston's eyes burned into her, and when she met that look, she could see the challenge within. He was wondering if she was going to rat him out. She should. She wanted to. She wanted to tell everyone what a dirty fucking liar he was, but she also didn't want to ruin everyone's vacation and have all the questions flying at her about what the fuck had happened.

Because she didn't even know what had happened. *How could any of this have happened to me?* She was used to being around players like that. She was used to model assholes. *God, hadn't I given my virginity to one of those assholes? Another fucking asshole to add to the list.*

Her face burned red at the thought. Everything seemed to fall into place at once—the phone calls when she had been over at Preston's place, him not responding to her late at night, him always having to work. She hadn't been looking for the signs because she felt safe with him, right with him. But she hadn't been safe at all, and here was the proof right before her eyes.

She didn't even know which way was up or down. She loved Preston. She wasn't ready for this to be over, but at the same time…she hated him, so viciously. She loved him as much as she hated him.

"So, tell us about him. Where is your boyfriend, Trihn?" Lydia asked.

"Yeah," Trihn murmured, ignoring her question. "Past tense."

"Past tense?" Lydia asked, confused.

"Yes. Past tense boyfriend."

As Lydia seemed to realize what Trihn had said, her face fell. "You guys aren't together anymore?"

"We broke up," she choked out. Her vision blurred as she stared at Preston. "He wasn't the guy that I thought he was."

"Oh, Trihn," Lydia said.

She placed her hand on Trihn's shoulders, and Trihn collapsed at her sympathy.

"I don't want to talk about it." She shrugged Lydia's arm away from her. "I'm going to call Renée. Just…give me some privacy."

Then, she barreled down the hallway, leaving the nightmare awaiting her behind. She needed to talk this out with someone. She needed to figure out what the hell to do about all of this.

Her feet carried her past the back deck, out to the trail to the beach, and all the way until her feet sank into the sand. She pulled her phone out and pressed the number for Renée as she hurried down the beach to the small cove where she and Ian had hidden away to escape the world when they were kids.

"You made it!" Renée said when she answered.

As soon as Trihn heard her best friend's voice, she burst into tears. Everything that she had been holding in rushed out of her. She was hiccuping over the sobs.

"Trihn! What's wrong? Are you okay? What happened? Oh my God, stop crying. Tell me what's going on!"

"Preston," she muttered through the tears.

"What about him?"

"He's here."

"What? Why?"

"He's…dating…Lydia."

There was silence on the other end.

"That motherfucker."

Trihn laughed hoarsely through the tears. "I know."

"How did this happen? Trihn, calm down. Breathe for me, hooker. You can't fall apart. You need to just breathe."

Trihn listened to her words and tried to follow her advice. *In through my nose, out through my mouth.* She closed her eyes and shut out everything, except for the sound of Renée's voice and the crash of the waves in the distance.

"Okay. Now, tell me everything."

So, Trihn spilled the whole sordid story of walking onto the property to find out that Lydia and Preston were together. She still couldn't quite believe that this was happening.

"So…have you talked to either of them about this?" Renée asked.

"No. It just happened. I was going to say something to Lydia, and then the words got stuck in my mouth. I was so shocked."

"I think you need to talk to Lydia," Renée said.

"What? Are you crazy? That is the *last* thing I need to do."

"I'm not crazy, Trihn. You're dating your sister's boyfriend! You need to talk to her."

Trihn covered her face with her free hand. "I don't know what to say. They started dating at the beginning of the summer. I can't even remember if I mentioned Lydia or anything to him. I seriously can't remember anything, except that I love him and I invited him here and he couldn't come because of work. Now, he's here with *her!*"

"What a douche bag!" Renée sighed. "Do you need me to come get you? I can borrow Matthews's car and drive out there."

Trihn swiped the tears off her face. Black mascara came off, and she didn't even want to know what she looked like. "I'm not going to make you drive all the way out here. And what would I even tell my parents? And Lydia…"

"Okay, I see your point," Renée conceded. "Lydia goes through men like most people go through socks. The likelihood that she's going to ditch him in a couple of weeks is really, really high."

"That doesn't make me feel any better!" Trihn cried into the phone.

"I know! But you're moving in with Lydia in three weeks. Three weeks," she repeated. "Just imagine that living situation if she finds out."

"Imagine the living situation if they stay together!"

"But what's the chance of that?" Renée asked.

"I don't know. All I know is that I cannot go back in there and look at them together. I know that he cheated on me and that he's cheating on her and that I hate him. But…I also thought I loved him. And if I tell Lydia what happened, then it will really be over with Preston."

Renée groaned. Trihn could practically hear her thoughts through the line.

Trihn didn't want to hear that it was over. She knew it was. *How could it ever be fixed after this?* But she wasn't ready for that.

"I guess just wait it out. I know it's torture, but wait until you and Lydia are alone, and you're not blindingly angry."

"What should I do in the meantime?" Trihn asked.

"Make him jealous?"

SIXTEEN

TRIHN STAYED HIDDEN AWAY IN HER ROOM.

There was no way that she was going to dinner. She wasn't ready to tell Lydia or confront Preston about what had happened, and she certainly wasn't ready to sit across from them at dinner. She could already hear them moving around in the room next door. She was sure Preston had his own room. He could at least be respectful enough to stay in it. She didn't even want to think about what they were doing in there.

She pulled her Bose headphones back out of her bag and enjoyed the wonderful noise-canceling capabilities. She thought she was successfully avoiding the world until her door swung inward, and she practically jumped out of her skin.

Her heart beat wildly as she was both terrified and hopeful that it would be Preston.

But as she dropped her headphones around her neck, Ian walked into the room. *Shit!* She had forgotten that she had invited him for dinner.

"Hey. What are you up to in here?" he asked, taking a casual step inside and leaning against the doorframe.

"Nothing. Listening to music."

He narrowed his eyes and tilted his head to the side as he examined her. "You okay?"

"Never been better," she lied.

"Really?"

Trihn cleared her throat and looked away from him. If he looked too closely at her, he would probably see what was churning inside of her.

"Are you carrying a sweater?" she asked, trying to force the joking tone back into her voice. "In August?"

"Don't try to change the subject," he said.

From where she sat, she could see that his ears were pink.

"Just come here."

"What?"

"Come here," he insisted.

Trihn left her headphones on the bed and walked across the room. "You'd better have a good reason for this, Peterson."

As soon as she was standing in front of him, he wrapped his arms around her waist and pulled her in for a tight hug. She didn't even know what to say. She stood there stiffly for a moment and then leaned into his chest, circling his waist. She breathed out heavily and tried to hold back the tears.

"It's going to be okay," he murmured.

She panicked for a split second, wondering how he knew what was going on.

But then he spoke again, "Your mom mentioned your breakup to me when I came in."

"Oh. Right."

She wished that were the real issue. That might be bearable compared to what was really going on.

Ian didn't have to say anything else though. They had known each other long enough for words not to matter. She had been there for him when his parents were going through issues. He had always been there when Lydia outshone Trihn and brought her pesky boyfriend on vacation. It was an easy friendship that Trihn appreciated more than ever at the moment.

Just as she was about to pull away, Lydia's door popped open, and Preston walked out of the room. He eyed them standing there in an embrace and raised his eyebrows. Whether from surprise or interest or jealousy, she didn't know.

Trihn quickly stepped away from Ian, her face burning. She couldn't even place the emotion hitting her head-on. She couldn't even look at Preston.

Thankfully, Ian stepped in. "You must be Lydia's new boyfriend."

He extended his hand, and Preston firmly shook it. *Was that too firmly? Could he be jealous? Of Ian of all people?*

Hypocrite.

"That's right. I'm Preston," he said. "And you are?"

"Ian Peterson. We live next door during the summer."

"I see."

135

Lydia stepped out of the room next. "Ready?" she asked, oblivious to what was going on in the hallway.

"Yeah, babe," Preston said. He put his arm around her waist and pulled her closer.

Trihn tried not to gag. Dinner was starting to sound like a horrible idea. Maybe she could just hang out in her room for the rest of break and pretend Preston wasn't here.

"You know, on second thought, I'm not really feeling that great. I'm going to pass on dinner. Sorry, Ian." Trihn started backing into her room.

"What?" Ian said. "No, come on, Trihn. You can't stay, locked away, in your room all night because some idiot broke up with you."

Before she had a chance to respond, Ian hauled her back out of her room and started forcing her down the hallway. She opened her mouth to protest but knew it wasn't going to work. Ian rarely put his foot down with her, and if he thought all that was wrong was some breakup, he wasn't going to change his mind.

"There you are!" her mother said when they walked into the dining room.

It was set for six, and her mother was already arranging dinner onto some fancy-looking china.

"Lasagna! Score!" Ian said. He took a seat next to her father, who was seated at the head of the table, reading on his iPad.

"Your favorite, if I remember," Linh said.

"Definitely."

Trihn bit her lip and slid into the spot next to Ian. For a split second before Preston took the chair in front of her, it'd felt like every other summer with just Trihn, Lydia, and Ian joking around and having a good time. Then, a pair of big blue eyes met her eyes from across the table, and that image disintegrated.

Trihn hastily looked away. Making eye contact was a bad idea.

Linh took her chair across from Gabriel with a smile. "Okay. Dig in!"

Food was passed around, and everyone filled their plates with Linh's amazing home-cooked food. Trihn stared down at her helping of lasagna. It was one of her favorites, too, but she didn't even have the stomach for it. She poked at it, swirling it around on her plate, before taking a small bite.

"So," Linh said, "are you two excited to start college in a couple of weeks?"

"Yes! I'm so ready to be back in the city," Ian said enthusiastically.

Trihn nodded halfheartedly. "Yeah. NYU is going to be...different."

"NYU is going to be wonderful," Lydia cried. "Just think, I'll be there, and Preston will be there! Renée and Ian will both be just uptown. I don't see how it could get any better."

"I guess." Trihn tried to imagine what college would look like next year, and all she visualized was static. "I was offered a job," she said, just to see what everyone would say.

"That's wonderful," Gabriel said.

"You won't have time for that!" Lydia cried.

"Another modeling gig?" her mother asked, brimming with excitement.

"No. Dancing," she said flatly.

"Dancing?" Lydia asked. She almost looked offended that Trihn would continue to pursue dance when Lydia never had. "With a company?"

Trihn let her eyes travel to Preston. He smirked when she glanced at him, and she remembered the recent night he had seen her perform at Slipper.

She swallowed hard. "You could say that."

"Well, as long as it doesn't interfere with school, it sounds like a good idea. Tell us more about it," Linh said.

"I don't have all the details yet," Trihn said.

"Look at my two daughters. Both motivated and independent young women."

Trihn tried not to roll her eyes, but Lydia just beamed across the table. After a minute of silence where everyone was digging into their food, Lydia glanced around and then finally settled on Trihn.

"*So*, what happened with your boyfriend?" Lydia asked.

Trihn met her gaze and just wanted to call her out for being a heartless bitch. Clearly, Trihn was fucking upset. *What the hell?*

"Lydia," Gabriel warned. Their father only butted in on rare occasions.

"What?" Lydia asked, acting all innocent. Loving, carefree Lydia would never be anything but a pleasant, caring, wonderfully meddlesome older sister who liked to stick her nose in other people's business.

"I really don't want to talk about it," Trihn ground out.

"You're just going to leave us hanging?"

"I said," Trihn snapped, dropping her fork, "I don't want to talk about it."

"Okay. Fine."

Linh cleared her throat and turned her attention away from the drama unfolding in front of her. "Ian, dear, you aren't dating anyone at the moment, are you?"

"No, ma'am," he said.

Trihn noticed how pink his ears were, and she just wanted to bury her face in her hands. This was even worse than she had expected, and Preston hadn't said a fucking word.

"And you'll be in Manhattan next year!"

Her mother's pretend innocent routine wasn't fooling anyone. It was clear what she was insinuating, and that was not going to happen.

"Mother!" she snapped. *How embarrassing!*

"Geez, Mom," Lydia piped in. "She's only been single a couple of hours, and already, you're trying to hook her up with the neighbor."

"I said nothing of the sort," Linh responded.

"I can't hear any more of this," Trihn said. "I can't even believe this is a topic of conversation."

"Well, this lasagna is delicious," Preston said, speaking up for the first time. All heads swiveled to him. "Thank you so much for the invitation, Mrs. Hamilton."

Trihn saw red. *Thanks for the invitation? Yeah. Thanks for the invitation to ruin my life.*

"Please call me Linh," her mother insisted.

"Mom, Preston is a marketing genius working for *Glitz* right now!"

"I didn't know you worked for the magazine," Linh said, clearly intrigued.

"Yeah. Well, I didn't realize you were related until very recently."

"Is that so?" Trihn asked. She leaned forward. "How recently?"

"What does it matter?" Lydia chimed in. "What matters is that he's so amazing that he should be *leading* the marketing team down there."

Trihn snorted. "He's entry-level for the summer."

"How do you know?" Lydia asked.

Trihn froze. *Oh, yeah.* "Some people can infer things, Ly. You're both doing work study."

"Well, I'm sure he's doing a fine job in marketing," Linh insisted.

"Anyone can be good at marketing," Trihn snapped.

"I couldn't," Ian said with a short laugh.

"But you're a genius at computers. See? This is what real skill looks like. Not just people who know how to twist words," Trihn said. She knew she was upset and on the verge of losing it, but she couldn't stop. "People will believe anything if you say it with enough conviction, isn't that right?" she spat Preston's words back at him.

His resulting smile only infuriated her more.

"God!" Lydia cried. "I know your boyfriend just broke up with you, but you are just being a bitch for no reason! You only dated him for a couple of weeks!"

Trihn's mouth dropped open, and then she shoved her chair back. "Excuse me, but I've suddenly lost my appetite."

"Trihn," Lydia murmured, as if realizing she had gone too far.

But Trihn didn't want to make up with Lydia. She didn't even want to look at Lydia. She saw Preston stamped all over her. Jealousy was a fiery inferno in her gut, and she had to hold back the tears as she stormed out of the room.

SEVENTEEN

"DO NOT OPEN THAT BOTTLE OF CHAMPAGNE," Ian said, lunging for Trihn across the cellar.

Pop.

"What did you say?" she asked coyly.

"My mom is going to kill me."

"Your mom won't even notice," Trihn insisted. She pressed the bottle to her lips and tipped it up in the air. "Oh my God, this is so good."

"Well, enjoy it. It's the last thing you'll ever drink."

"You're so dramatic."

"It's her favorite!" He winced.

"Then, I guess we have to drink the whole bottle before the party and stash the evidence, huh?" she asked. The logic seemed sound to her.

Ian gave her a skeptical look but took the bottle when she passed it to him. There was no going back now. They couldn't recork the bottle or anything at this point.

"You're going to be the death of me." But he drank from the bottle without another word.

At least she was getting him to drink.

The last three days Trihn had stayed over at Ian's house to escape the insanity that was happening at her place. She couldn't stand another second of Preston and Lydia being together or her mother trying to make her feel better by forcing her on Ian or really anything at the moment. Mostly, she had spent her days in a haze of inebriation by the pool. Margaritas, daiquiris, mojitos…vodka, rum, gin…and even a few Coronas for good measure—anything to keep her tipsy enough not to give a shit.

But she couldn't avoid the Petersons' party.

Ian's parents would throw a huge party every year, and their friends from all over would come to the Hamptons to celebrate. It was one of the biggest events of the season. Trihn should be looking forward to seeing the friends that she and Ian had made over the years, but all she could think about was confronting Preston and Lydia.

"So, are you going to tell me why you've really been spending every minute over here this week?" Ian asked. He placed the expensive bottle of champagne on the bar next to him.

"I don't know what you mean. I always spend time over here."

"Yeah," he agreed. "But it's normally not this much, and some of the time, Lydia is usually here with whatever new guy she's been seeing."

"So?"

"So...I was there for that awkward dinner conversation. What's with you and Ly? Do you just hate the new guy? Are you worried about sharing her time when you get to NYU? What's up? I know something other than the breakup has been simmering," he said intuitively.

Trihn grabbed the champagne back off the bar and took another swig. "Can we not talk about this? I'd rather just keep drinking and dancing."

She took his hand in hers and forced him to twirl her around in place.

"You *know* I can't dance."

Trihn laughed. "You can when you've had a little bit more to drink. Here. Drink up."

He retrieved the bottle that she'd practically launched at him. "I don't consider that dancing."

"What is it then, Ian?" she teased. "Sex on the dance floor?"

His whole face burned at the comment. "I know you're just trying to change the subject."

"What's wrong with that?" she asked, turning away from him.

He set the bottle back down, grabbed her shoulders in his hands, and stopped her in place. "Because I know something is bothering you. I can't fix it unless I know what it is, and I hate when I can't fix a problem."

"I'm not a computer, Ian. You can't fix me," she said calmly. But her heart was racing. No one could fix what had happened.

"I know, but you're not the problem. Something is bothering you, and I can fix it. Why won't you tell me what it is?" he demanded.

She saw a fire in Ian that he didn't normally bring out. He must be really worried. Normally, he was so shy that he would never demand anything from her.

"Preston is cheating on Lydia," she spat out.

Ian dropped his arms and stared at her in surprise. "What? How do you know?"

"Because I saw him with someone else."

"You did?"

"Yeah. I saw him in the city."

"Are you sure it was Preston? I mean, there are nearly nine million people in New York City. It could have just been someone who looked like him," Ian insisted.

"It was him."

"You're certain?"

"Ian, yes." She had never been more certain in her life. But the words that *she* was the person he had been cheating with somehow got stuck in her mouth. He had been cheating on both of them. They'd had a relationship. He had been her boyfriend, too, not just Lydia's.

Now, Trihn was just…empty.

"You must not have told Lydia."

"No, I haven't."

"Are you going to?"

She nodded. Yeah, she had every intention of telling Lydia as soon as they weren't all locked together in this insufferable house. Just a few more days, and then Lydia could know the truth.

"I will when we get home."

"Maybe we should go tell her now. She deserves to know the kind of scumbag she's dating."

Trihn blanched. "Give me that bottle back."

He grabbed it and held it high over her head, and even though she was tall, there was no way she was going to be able to reach it.

"We should go tell Lydia."

"*We?*" Trihn asked. "No, I'm not going to tell her, Ian. Definitely not right now while we're here with him. She's never going to believe me, especially after that catastrophe of a dinner. You heard her call me a bitch. She's just going to think I'm jealous."

Ian lowered the champagne bottle as he considered her words. "Are you sure Lydia would do that?"

Trihn leveled him with a flat look and snatched the bottle back from him. "You know Lydia."

"Yeah, I do," he conceded. "She probably would go ballistic."

"I know." Trihn brought the bottle to her lips again. "By the way, you're going to need to help me finish this."

They finished that bottle and started in on another—cheaper—bottle.

By the time the party was in full swing, Trihn was in her new favorite place—abandon.

She had gone home only long enough to change into her new emerald-green dress that she had bought for just this occasion, and she'd reassured her mother that she was going to the party. She had stayed home long enough to listen to her mother go on about how she wasn't spending any time with the family, and then she'd left. And she'd convinced herself she was drunk enough that she didn't care that Preston was stealing her last family vacation before she would go to college.

Everyone who was anybody showed up at the Petersons' that night. The parents were congregating inside and on the deck of the house while the younger generation had ended up in the pool and down on the beach. Most of the people near Trihn's age were even further gone than she was, and she was pretty sure a good number of them were on something much stronger than alcohol.

Not that she cared tonight.

Music was pumping through some high-tech surround-sound speakers that made the sounds reach all the way out to the beach. Her feet were in the sand, her hands were over her head, and she was dancing to the tempo with a few girls. They were a giggly mess and kept falling over into the sand. As Trihn tried to help one girl stand up, the girl yanked on her arm and pulled her down next to her.

"Oh my God," Trihn cried. She had sand all over her new dress.

The girl just laughed. "Sorry, Trihn. Stronger than I look I guess."

"Sure you are."

She was trying to get to her feet again when someone bent down and put an arm around her waist.

"Let me help you."

Trihn looked up into Preston's eyes, and her body went slack. He was touching her. Her head swam, and all she could think about was how amazing his lips looked and how much she wanted to kiss him and all the dirty things those lips had done to her body.

He smiled down at her, as if he could read her thoughts.

He hoisted her up easily onto her shaky legs and pulled her against him. She wasn't breathing properly.

His skin burned her everywhere it touched her, and all she wanted to do was lean into him. This was right, one hundred and fifty percent right.

"I like the dress," he breathed.

Then, she came to her senses. This was not right. There was no way this would ever be right again. "Get away from me," she said, wrenching out of his grip.

"Hey, hey, hey," Ian said. He jogged up to them and put a protective arm around Trihn. "You okay?"

"Fine."

"You should leave her alone," Ian said.

Preston's eyebrows rose. "I was just helping her up out of the sand."

"Yeah, well, I think you've helped enough," Ian spat back at Preston.

"Come on, Ian. Let's just go get another drink," she said.

"I'm not sure another drink is in your best interest," he said as they left Preston standing alone.

"After that, I'm almost certain it is."

Once they reached the bar, Trihn grabbed the first thing she could and downed the drink in one long chug.

"Whoa! Slow down."

She wiped her mouth and trashed the drink. Grabbing another in her hand, she veered back out into the sand and headed straight toward Lydia.

"Trihn, what are you doing?" Ian asked, following her.

"I'm going to tell everyone what an asshole Preston really is."

"Right now?" he squeaked.

They had almost made it all the way to where Lydia and Preston were standing when Ian grabbed Trihn around the waist and held her back.

Her back was flush against his chest, and he leaned down, so he could whisper into her ear, "You are making a horrible mistake."

"Ian," she growled, "let me go."

"You didn't think Lydia would believe you when you were sober. What makes you think that she's going to believe you when you're drunk?" Ian prodded.

Trihn deflated at his words. Of course he was right.

She relaxed back into him with a frustrated sigh. "I just want it to be over."

"Not tonight."

Lydia noticed them standing a short distance away. She laughed and waved. "Well, I never thought I'd see the day when Mom's prodding worked."

"What?" Trihn asked. She took a step forward but stumbled as all the alcohol seemed to hit her at once.

"You and Ian." Lydia suggestively raised her eyebrows.

Preston stared between them with his eyes narrowed. "Nice rebound."

Trihn's mouth opened and then closed. She was *not* interested in Ian. *What the hell is wrong with them?*

"Hey, it's okay. You can like whoever you want," Lydia said. "Free love, sis." Then, she turned back to Preston and left Trihn standing there in shock.

"Trihn," Ian said.

He reached for her, but she took another step away from him.

Oh, shit! Does he think that I like him, too? Her head hurt at that thought. He couldn't think that. No one should even be thinking that. He was just Ian. And she was just Trihn. And she was still dealing with the Preston thing to even consider that Ian might actually like her..

"I need some fresh air."

"You're outside," he pointed out.

"Fresh air…away from everyone else."

"Including me?"

As she started walking toward her house, Ian followed.

"Including everyone," Trihn said. "I just…want to be alone."

His face fell.

Oh, no. He didn't like her. He couldn't like her. He had just been trying to take care of her. There was nothing else to it.

She just needed fresh air to think and try to come down from how drunk she was. At least that was what she was going to tell herself.

EIGHTEEN

TRIHN DIDN'T MAKE IT INSIDE.

Her head swam, and she figured the pool deck was far enough. It was empty and secluded. She could still hear the party raging next door, but six-foot-high shrubs and an Olympic-size pool separated their houses, so it was muffled at least. The air didn't feel as constricted here.

No Preston. No Lydia. No Ian. No questioning everything.

Trihn lay down on one of the cushioned benches next to the hot tub, propped her feet up on the white wooden armrest, and stared up at the stars above her.

Solace. Sweet solace. Just me and the universe.

This was the good thing about alcohol. She didn't have to think or feel or really do anything. She could just lie here all night.

Then, hands covered her eyes, blocking her view of the stars, and she screamed.

One of the hands moved to cover her mouth, and a soft whisper came from behind her, "Shh."

Trihn tried to scream again.

Then, his voice filtered through her struggle. "Calm down, beautiful."

She would recognize that voice anywhere.

Preston.

He released her when she stopped struggling.

She quickly sat up, bringing a wave of dizziness with her. "What…are you doing here?"

"Came looking for you."

She reached out for the bench to steady herself and took a deep breath. She needed a clear head for this conversation. "Why? I don't know what you want."

"I wanted to see you," he said smoothly.

His eyes scanned her body, and her heart accelerated, but at the same time, she was disgusted. *How can he look at me like that? And why do I want him to?*

She was drawn to him like a moth to a flame.

Those dark blue eyes dancing in the dim deck light, the strong jaw and messily styled hair that she wished her fingers were running through, the loose khakis and blue-striped button-up he had rolled up to his elbows—everything about him made her ache to move closer toward him. But she stayed rooted in place.

"What the fuck, Preston? You're dating my sister!" Trihn hissed.

"Last I checked, I was dating you, too."

"That's disgusting!" she spat. "We're not together. I don't even know how you could date two people at once like that!"

"You seemed pretty cozy with Ian. I thought this was par for the course with you."

Her mouth dropped open. "Ian and I are just friends. Always have been and always will be."

"That's not what it looked like to me."

She shook her head. "Don't try to put this on me. Even if I were dating Ian, which I'm not," she clarified, "you and I were over the second I saw you with her."

"Yes, I think you tried to clarify that when you said your boyfriend broke up with you. Clever lie." He smirked and reached out for her, as if none of that was of any concern. His fingers wrapped around her waist, and he drew her to him.

"Don't touch me." She wrenched out of his grasp and crossed her arms. She wobbled on her feet and then steadied herself on the bench again. "You lost any right you had to touch me."

"Then, why haven't you told anyone?" he asked. He cocked his head to the side to examine her.

"I…" She closed her mouth. Nothing she could say would justify why she hadn't told Lydia. She didn't think Lydia would believe her. She didn't want to ruin the vacation. She worried it would ruin everything. Her heart was shattering into a million pieces, and she wasn't prepared for it to be really over.

"Yes?" he asked.

"How long have you known that Lydia and I are related?" she blurted out.

"Since you told me that Linh Hamilton was your mother," he answered easily. "I hadn't really considered the possibility until then."

"That was so…long ago," she stammered.

"Two weeks," he offered.

"And you didn't think that you should maybe fucking tell someone about it?" she asked, her anger heating again like a flame to a fuse. "God, you're just a cheating bastard!"

"Trihn, you're asking all the wrong questions."

"Are you insane?" she asked. The adrenaline from this conversation was burning off the alcohol in her system, and she stood a little straighter. "Is *that* a better question?"

"I'm not. I just fell for two incredible women for two very different reasons."

He slowly started walking closer to her. She felt like she had lead in her feet because, even as he approached her, she didn't move away. She wasn't sure if she even could at that point.

He stopped before her with just inches between them and brushed a stray strand of hair off her face. "How could I resist you after that first introduction?"

Trihn remembered that fateful day when she had met Preston. She hadn't been able to tear her eyes away from him, and he was the first person she had really wanted to pursue. He had given her the confidence to push for a relationship, and then he had pulled the rug out from beneath her.

As her mind went back to that day, standing on Lydia's steps, she gasped. "You were visiting Lydia! That's why you were there that day!" she accused.

He smirked, as if knowing all the puzzle pieces were finally falling into place.

"The only reason I know you is because of Lydia." She shook her head in disbelief. Pure anger shot through her emerald-green eyes. "How could you do this, Preston? You could have let it be that day, but you pursued me. You showed up at the studio. You took me to the ballet. You were the one who bribed someone, so we could go backstage and fool around. You were the one who fucked me at your place, at the studio after-hours, at—"

"I know what we did."

"And you've been sleeping with her," Trihn accused.

"Trihn…"

But she wouldn't listen to what he had to say. Preston's fingers dug into her hips, holding her in place, and they weren't gentle. She could tell just by that action that he wanted her.

And she wanted him. He was supposed to be special…to be hers. Trihn had waited. Fuck, she had wanted it to feel right. And, of course, it had felt right with Preston, who belonged to someone else. And not just anyone else…to Lydia.

"I hate you," she spat.

His smile grew wider. "But I thought you *loved* me."

Her mouth dropped open. Without thinking, she pulled her hand back and smacked him as hard as she could across the face. His head whipped to the side. There was a moment of silence after the slap rang through the air where Preston looked off to the side and fumed. Then, he turned to look at her again.

Her chest was heaving. She couldn't believe she had done that. She had never slapped anyone before. She had never been violent.

His eyes were shining bright, and whatever ounce of control he had held on to was shattered in that look. His mouth crashed down on hers. Even if she had wanted to stop him, she wouldn't have been able to. The white gloves were off.

Soon, they were in a frenzy, tearing at each other's clothes, desperate for the feel of skin on skin, as the tension cracked like lightning between them.

His pants fell around his ankles. Her thong was tossed to the side, and then he shoved her short green dress up around her hips. She bit down on his lip as he manhandled her into place. She ran her fingers through the hair she had been daydreaming about and then tugged to the point of pain. He grunted but didn't stop. He just pushed her backward onto the bench she had just been lying on.

"You want it rough, don't you?" he growled before covering her body.

He spread her legs open before him, and then he reached behind her, roughly grabbed her ass, and positioned himself in front of her.

"I hate you," she barked out.

"Keep telling yourself that," he said as he shoved inside her.

She cried out, and he just covered her mouth with his to muffle the sound of her screams, but it hardly masked the sound of their bodies slapping together.

And he was as rough as he'd promised to be. Pinioning her arms above her head, he savagely thrust into her. Their conflicting emotions fueled their passion. She loved him, and she hated him. She wanted him to fuck her senseless. She wanted him and despised him. She couldn't stop even if she wanted to…and she didn't. She just wanted him.

"I want to give it to you deeper," he told her.

She didn't resist as he pulled out in one quick motion, gripped her hips, and flipped her over, so she was on all fours in front of him.

"That's better," he said, smacking her ass hard with his open palm.

She shot forward as pain blossomed on the spot. He dug into her hips, bringing her back toward him, and then reentered her.

As he started pumping again, his hand twisted around her long mane of hair and tugged until her head was looking upward. Then, he buried himself inside of her. She squirmed against him. Even in her addled brain, it was borderline uncomfortable. He was hitting so deep, but the pain and pleasure mingled when he started moving again. He drew all the way out and then slammed back into her.

After a few agonizingly slow repetitions, she thought she was going to combust. He didn't seem too far off. Their bodies moved in time. She pushed back into him as he forced his way in over and over again.

Their breathing was labored, and then she felt it. Everything happened at once. He started coming, and her body responded with her own orgasm. She shuddered, and her hands gave out beneath her. He released her hair and was holding on to her hips as he finished.

After a few seconds of heavy breathing, Preston slid out of her and started to right himself. "That was..." he said, trailing off.

"Amazing?" she ventured, flipping over.

"Yeah. Amazing."

Trihn slid her dress back down her hips and stood. She wished that she could blame what had happened on the alcohol she had consumed today, but she knew it had nothing to do with the reality of the situation. While she had been tipsy, she had been coherent and would have gone through with it sober.

She knew what she had done and how wrong it was. And with every look at Preston…she hated him a little bit more for it.

"Good, because that's the last time you'll *ever* get that again," she said.

She walked back toward her house, leaving him all alone, without a backward glance. She knew she would torture herself later, but for now, she just needed to hold her head high and get out of there.

One day, that bastard would realize what he was missing.

NINETEEN

THUMP. THUMP. THUMP.

Trihn peeled her eyes open and frowned. She had a splitting headache, and the noise wasn't helping anything. It was a consistent boom against the wall at the head of her bed. And it wasn't going away.

Seriously, what the fuck is that?

She wiped sleep out of her eyes and slowly eased into a sitting position. The noise had pulled her from a dream, leaving her disoriented. Last night was a blur of bad decisions. She hadn't returned to the party. Instead, she had gone back to her room and passed out to try to forget what had happened.

Looking at the alarm clock on the nightstand showed her that it was still too early for her to be awake. The thumping stopped, and Trihn sighed back into her pillow. She would just get a few more hours of sleep before she thought about what the morning would bring.

"Yes!" a scream split through the wall. "Yes. Yes. Fuck, yes."

Thump. Thump. Thump.

Trihn bolted upright. Her eyes snapped open. She ignored the stab of pain in her skull as realization dawned on her. She knew *exactly* what that sound was.

But no…he wouldn't. There was no way. She couldn't believe it. Her mouth went dry as the noise escalated in the other room.

Oh, but he would. He would absolutely have sex with Lydia in her room next to Trihn's the morning after having just had sex with Trihn. That was exactly what he had been doing the whole time she was dating him.

She was so angry that her hands shook. She wanted nothing more than to wring his neck.

And cry. Crying seemed like a viable alternative.

But her tear ducts were dry. She didn't want to shed a tear for him anyway. She just wanted to hold on to this anger. This anger would drive her, fuel her, rather than crumple her and make her collapse under the weight of the deception.

She had known how wrong it was to let Preston fuck her last night. It was an infinite amount of wrong. She had walked away, knowing that it was the end—the official end at least.

But she hadn't thought that meant he would be fucking her sister the next morning. It hadn't even been twelve hours, and already, he was getting off with someone else.

Trihn jumped out of bed and threw on shorts and a T-shirt. She slipped into a pair of sandals, grabbed her backpack and headphones, and then rushed out of her room. She noisily slammed the door behind her. Hopefully, they would realize that she had heard, and they would feel bad about it, but she knew Preston wouldn't. He probably wouldn't even stop. Nothing could change the fact that she had heard it anyway.

She trotted down the stairs two at a time and went through the kitchen. She had almost made it to the back door when her mother stopped her.

"Trihn, is that you?" Linh called.

"Yeah, Mom. Just going over to Ian's," Trihn called back.

"Wait, just one minute."

Trihn sighed and slunk back into the kitchen. "What?"

Linh raised her eyebrows. "What's with the attitude?"

"Just on my way out."

"That's fine, but don't spend the whole week over there. Ian will be in the city next year, and you can spend your time with him then. We're going out on the sailboat later, and you two should join the family."

"Ian and I aren't together, Mom," she quickly clarified.

"No one said you were."

Trihn snorted and started walking away. "Everyone is just insinuating it."

Linh shrugged her shoulders. "He's a nice boy."

"Ugh! Mom!"

"Fine. I'll see you two later, but please try to change into something more suitable for the boat."

Trihn rolled her eyes and quickly left the house. The last thing she wanted to do was go on a sailboat with her family and Preston. Besides the fact that no one going on that sailboat should be wearing fucking white, she couldn't handle another family outing. She couldn't handle Lydia. She couldn't handle Preston. She just wanted *out*.

And *out* was the only thing she was thinking about as she dashed across the yard and over to the Petersons' house. She didn't bother knocking. Even though it was early, she knew Ian had likely been up, gone for his morning run, and eaten breakfast. It was his MO. Didn't matter that he had drunk nearly as much as her last night. He was a stand-up guy.

She found him back on the patio. His parents were seated around the table. His mother was carefully slicing a grapefruit while his father read the paper. Ian had his computer in front of him and was typing away at the speed of light.

"Hey," she said when she walked in on them.

Ian's head shot up. He had circles under his eyes, like he hadn't gotten any sleep last night. Or maybe he was hungover. She had never seen him hungover, but it was possible.

"Trihn," he said. His voice was calm and controlled with none of the playful tone she had heard from him every day this week.

"Hi," she said cautiously. "Hello, Mr. and Mrs. Peterson."

"Trihn," Mr. Peterson said, not looking up from his paper.

"Good to see you again, dear," Betty said.

"Can I talk to you?" she asked Ian. She tilted her head to the side, gesturing for them to go inside.

He answered by closing his computer and walking past her into the house.

Once they were in the den, Trihn fidgeted from side to side. She didn't normally feel uncomfortable around Ian, but something was definitely off. He hadn't really even looked at her since he had gotten up from the table.

"So, what's up?" Trihn asked.

She wanted to launch into what had happened this morning and freak out. She wanted to cry and scream and have someone who actually cared listen, but she didn't do any of that. Instead, she just stood awkwardly and waited for him to say something.

"You're the one who came over," he said.

"Yeah. And you're the one not looking at me."

Ian glanced up into her eyes, and she saw pain. He was in pain. Both of them were—though clearly for different reasons.

"Now, I'm looking at you."

"Okay," she said. "Are you mad at me?"

"Mad?" he asked in disbelief. "That's not the word I would use."

"I don't understand."

"Don't you?" he demanded.

She shrugged her shoulders.

"You told me that Preston was cheating on Lydia. You made me hate the guy. But you didn't tell me that he was cheating on her with *you*."

Trihn's mouth dropped open. "What?"

"I saw you last night!" he cried, the words erupting out of him, as if he was releasing a caged animal.

Trihn stood stark still. "When?" Her voice was so quiet.

"You know when."

"I—"

"You had sex with him, Trihn!" His hands visibly shook. "On the pool deck where anyone could just walk up and see you two together. And guess who did just that?"

"I don't know what to say," she whispered.

"What were you thinking?"

"I wasn't."

"Clearly!" Ian was barely keeping it together.

Trihn covered her face with her hands and shook her head. She could not do this right now, not with Preston and Lydia having sex next door while her whole world crumbled down around her.

"We were dating," she told him.

"What?" Ian asked in confusion.

"Preston is the guy I was dating before I got here. We didn't break up." She looked back up at him. "I just said that when I saw him with Lydia because I didn't know they were dating…or really that he was dating anyone else. I was blindsided, and then I didn't know how to tell her. Everything swiftly got out of control."

"Oh."

"Yeah." Trihn sighed and sank down into a chair.

"I still can't fucking believe you had sex with him last night," Ian said. He crossed his arms over his chest.

"You and me both."

"Were you just wasted? Is that why you acted so stupid?"

She shook her head. She deserved that. "No. I was tipsy for sure, but I knew what I was doing."

"You could have found me last night and told me the truth about Preston. Instead, you went to him," Ian said. He sounded so disgusted with her. "What the fuck? You can't say you were ignorant then. You knew that he was with Lydia."

"I know! I didn't go to him," she said. "He found me, and I was just stupid enough not to walk away."

"Unbelievably stupid!"

"I know how this must all seem, but I was in love with him, Ian. I thought we were going to be together when I moved into the city in a couple of weeks."

"That doesn't excuse you from having sex with him last night," he said.

Trihn winced. "No, it doesn't."

"I was here for you, Trihn. All week, I consoled you over this guy who had broken up with you, being everything you needed. Then, you went and fucked him anyway."

"I know, okay?" she yelled back. "Don't you think I've already been beating myself up enough about this? I feel like absolute shit for letting that happen. I am well aware that it's the dumbest thing I've ever done in my life. God! But it doesn't mean that I'm not hurting! Not to mention the fact that he is *fucking* my sister in her room at this very moment," she said, standing and pointing toward her house. "I just want *out*. I want away from here and away from them."

"There's nowhere you can escape to, Trihn. You're going to have to deal with them eventually."

"But not today, okay?" she pleaded. "Can we just…go away?"

"Where?" he asked skeptically.

"Will you just take me home?"

"Home? Next door or home…"

"The city."

Ian sighed heavily. "I don't think it's a good idea to just run away from this."

"If I don't deal with it, maybe it will just go away?"

"I don't think so."

"Me either."

Trihn sat and curled in on herself. She knew what she needed to do. She needed to talk to Lydia and get everything out in the open, but the thought of that was debilitating.

"Just think…he expects you to stay silent. He expects to just get away with this," Ian told her. "Are you going to let him?"

Trihn shook her head and steeled her resolve. "No."

TWENTY

TRIHN TOOK A HESITANT STEP back inside her house. Preparations were being made all around her for the sailing trip her mother had planned. She and Ian had discussed what she was going to say to Lydia, but it hadn't made her feel any better. In fact, she felt awful. Her stomach ached, and at any second, she might be sick. She knew that she needed to talk to Lydia, but that didn't make it any easier.

"There you are!" Linh said when she saw Trihn tiptoeing around. "Just in time. We're leaving in half an hour, so go change."

"Have you seen Lydia?"

"She's tanning out back. Will you tell her that she needs to get moving, too?"

"Sure," Trihn agreed easily.

She took a deep breath. The knot in her stomach hardened, and she was shaking by the time she made it to the back door. She didn't know what she was going to find when she got there. She just prayed that Preston wasn't going to be there because the last thing she wanted was to have this conversation in front of him.

No, she wouldn't be able to have this conversation with him around. He would twist her words. It didn't matter that she had loved him. She knew firsthand what he was capable of. She had experienced it last night on the very pool deck she was looking at now.

She tried to quell the tremble running through her body. It didn't help that it was a perfect day. *Couldn't it match my mood or something?* But no. No rain on the forecast, a perfect cloudless day, and the whole merry family was supposed to go out sailing.

Not after she got this over with.

Trihn pushed opened the back door and stepped outside. She could see Lydia lying facedown on a lounge chair in an all white bathing suit. Her blonde hair cascaded over the side of the lounger while she read a magazine. Trihn's gaze shifted to survey the rest of the pool deck, but she found it empty, no Preston in sight. That was a relief. But it didn't necessarily mean he wasn't nearby.

"Hey," Trihn said hesitantly. She approached her sister on the deck. *God, can I actually go through with this?*

Lydia's head popped up. She rested her elbows on the lounge chair and smiled at her sister. "There you are! Are you ready to go sailing? It's been so long since we went. I can't wait!"

"I don't know, Ly."

"You don't know what?" she asked, rolling over onto her back and sitting up. "You *have* to go with us. It's tradition. Mom is going to have a fit if you try to back out."

"I'm not sure I'm feeling up for it."

"It's because you're in those dark colors you're always wearing. Come on, Trihn. Black and studs and dark denim for the beach? I have the cutest outfit you can borrow for the boat."

A smile tugged at the corner of Trihn's lips. *Why couldn't Lydia act like this all the time?* This was the sister who Trihn missed and who she was looking forward to moving in with in a couple of weeks. This was the sister who shouldn't have her heart broken.

"That sounds nice," Trihn said softly.

"Plus, Ian will die when he sees you in it."

"Ugh!" Trihn groaned. "Ian and I are not together."

"But he wants you! I know, in your world, it's bad to rebound or whatever, but in my world, you say good-bye to one and hello to the next. Give it a try. I know Ian would go crazy if you did. He's liked you since you were kids."

"What?" Trihn asked, laughing because of her sister's ridiculous ideals. "He has not."

"Please! You are not that naive."

"I…wait, what?"

"Ian likes you. He always has. But you totally friend-zoned him in middle school," Lydia explained. "That doesn't mean you can't unfriend-zone him. He's cute, and you guys get along. He's serious. He's smart. You'll both be in the city." Lydia waggled her eyebrows up and down. "Think about it."

And she was. Thinking about it made her gag. "He's like a brother to me. Just no. No way."

Lydia sighed heavily and sagged back in her chair. "Your loss. I bet he would worship the ground you walked on."

Trihn shook her head. She wished that she and Lydia could just keep talking about frivolous things and let their relationship seamlessly repair itself on its own. That was what Trihn and Renée had talked about when she had first found out that Lydia was dating Preston. Lydia would probably break up with him in a couple of weeks, and then all would be well again between them.

But after last night and this morning...could I really wait around for that to happen? Pretend like it didn't bother me? Pretend like Lydia didn't need to know the truth?

"This isn't really why I came out here," Trihn said. She swallowed hard and tried to meet her sister's eyes.

"Oh, yeah? Did Mom send you to tell me to make sure I got ready?"

"Well, yeah. She did, but—"

"All ready!" Lydia said, spreading her arms wide. She hopped out of her chair. "I don't need more than bathing suit, but you on the other hand need my help. Come on. Let's try that outfit on you." Lydia latched on to her arm and tried to drag her inside.

"Lydia, I need to talk to you."

"Okay. Let's talk while you try on the outfit."

"Lydia," Trihn complained, "can't we talk first?"

"Why so serious?" Lydia said in her best impersonation of the Joker. Then, she was dragging Trihn through the house and back to their bedrooms. She opened the door and tugged Trihn inside.

Trihn froze when she entered.

There was the bed, Lydia's huge king-size bed.

It was freshly made, so the maid service must have already come through this morning, but it didn't erase the memories. Lydia and Preston had had sex on this bed this morning. Trihn's stomach revolted at the thought.

"Is…is Preston around?"

"No," Lydia said. She was rummaging through the closet, and then she pulled out a white flowy skirt and a blue-and-white striped tank. She tossed them to Trihn. "Try it on."

Trihn sighed and then stripped out of her outfit and into the ensemble Lydia had given her.

"Anyway, Preston has been on the phone with work all morning. He's supposed to be taking the time off, but his boss keeps bothering him with this project he's been working on."

Sure he is.

"I see."

At least he wasn't around to interrupt them.

Lydia shoved Trihn in front of the full-length mirror and smiled. "Perfect. Ian will die."

"Lydia," Trihn said.

"I know you're not together." Lydia put her hands up in the air.

Trihn wrinkled her nose. She had to admit that the outfit did look nice even if it wasn't something she would normally wear. But her face fell when she realized that, all this time, she had just been avoiding the conversation that she knew she needed to have.

"What's that look?" Lydia asked.

"What look?"

"Whatever is on your face right now."

171

Trihn turned away from the mirror. "I said that we needed to talk. It's about Preston."

Lydia huffed loudly and rolled her eyes. "Of course it is. It's always something. I really don't know what's been up with you on this trip, Trihn. Mom and Dad think you're just being a hormonal teenager, but I think it's something else. Normally, you're the serious one, and I'm the happy-go-lucky one, and then everything works out. But this trip, you've been just so mad at the world. Everyone is kind of over it," Lydia told her. "Just because your boyfriend broke up with you doesn't mean that you have to take it out on everyone else."

Trihn clenched her hands into fists at her sides. Everything she had been planning to say flittered out of her mind. "My boyfriend didn't break up with me."

"What do you mean?"

"He didn't break up with me. I just said that when I saw him with you. I didn't want this to happen this way, Ly, but Preston is—or was my boyfriend."

Lydia's eyes rested on Trihn for a second before she doubled over. She was laughing so hard that tears brimmed her eyes. She patted her chest twice and then coughed. "Oh, that's a good one, Trihn."

"I'm not joking," Trihn said.

"Oh, please! Don't be ridiculous."

"I'm not being ridiculous either, Lydia. I'm telling you that I dated Preston," she said, trying to get through to her sister.

Lydia crossed her arms over her chest and stood nearly nose-to-nose with Trihn. "I get that you're upset because I brought Preston along, but I'm not stupid. Your boyfriend broke up with you, and now, you're taking that out on everyone else. I've seen the way you've been looking at Preston this whole trip. You're clearly jealous."

"You know what? You're right," Trihn said, throwing her hands out. "My boyfriend, Preston, has been dating someone else. As you can imagine, that makes me pretty jealous."

"Stop saying that!" Lydia cried. "Preston never dated you!"

"I really wish that were true," Trihn told her. "I wish that this trip were the first time I'd ever met him, but it's not. Preston and I met on the front steps of your building a couple of months ago. After running into me that day, he pursued me, and we've been together all summer. I never knew he was seeing you. I actually didn't even know *you* were seeing anyone until Mom told me you were bringing your boyfriend on vacation with us."

"If all of this is true," Lydia said doubtfully, "then why is this the first I'm hearing about it?"

Trihn sighed and hugged herself to avoid the words she hated to say. "I was blindsided at first, so I didn't want to lash out from anger, but then I think a part of me wanted to believe that you guys would just break up, like you do with everyone else. Trust me, I didn't even want to tell you right now, but I thought you deserved to know."

With those final words, it seemed to hit Lydia. Her face fell, her shoulders drooped, and she looked like someone had just socked her in the stomach. "So…you're saying that Preston has been cheating on me this whole time?"

Trihn nodded reluctantly.

"And you, too."

"Yeah." Trihn wrung her hands in front of her.

"I just can't believe…" Lydia's words trailed off as she looked over Trihn's shoulder. "Hey," she whispered.

"Hey, babe," Preston said. He leaned against the doorframe. "What's going on in here?"

"We were just talking," Lydia said. "And I was giving Trihn an outfit for sailing."

Preston glanced at Trihn's outfit. "Nice." He walked over to Lydia and planted a kiss on her cheek.

Trihn tried not to cringe.

"Sorry it took so long, but I'm all yours now. Work just really needed me."

"Oh, yeah? What's her name?" Trihn said under her breath.

Preston's eyes narrowed, and this time, Trihn winked before turning and walking out of the room.

She could hear Lydia yelling at him from down the hall.

TWENTY-ONE

Trihn should have felt better.

But she didn't. Telling Lydia the truth didn't change the fact that Preston had slept with and cheated on both of them. Really, nothing had changed, except now both she and Lydia were suffering for what he had done. Trihn hated that her sister had to hurt with her, but she knew telling her was the right thing to do.

Trihn trudged back down the stairs on her way to Ian's house, but her mother stopped her in the foyer.

"Trihn, I love that outfit!" Linh called. She smiled at her from the kitchen where a large picnic basket sat on the counter with a half-empty bottle of chardonnay next to it.

"Oh. Thanks." She had forgotten that she was still decked out in the outfit that Lydia had wanted her to wear for sailing. "Lydia let me borrow it."

"It'll be perfect for the boat." She took a long sip out of the glass of wine in front of her.

"Mom—"

"Is Lydia about ready to go? Your father is restless to get out on the water, and you know how he is when he gets restless."

"Yeah, I do, but I don't think Lydia is going to go sailing," Trihn told her.

"What?" Linh asked. She set her wine down and looked up at her in surprise. "Why not? She was looking forward to it. It's her favorite thing to do at the beach."

"Yeah. Um…she and Preston are arguing."

Linh frowned. She glanced up the stairs like she wanted to go up there and find out what was going on. "Is it serious?"

Trihn nodded. "I heard her yelling in her room from down the hall."

"Did you hear what it's about?"

"Um…no," Trihn lied. She definitely didn't want her mother weighing in on the Lydia-Preston-Trihn fiasco.

"Should I go up there and check on her?"

"I think it would probably be best if you didn't. We should give them some privacy and go sailing."

Linh pursed her lips. "All right. I don't want to interfere, but they seemed fine this morning."

Don't I know it?

"Okay. Well, go get Ian, and then we'll head out."

"Oh, Mom—"

"If your sister can't go, then you absolutely have to go. March right over to the Petersons' and tell Ian that we need him. I'm not doing all the heavy lifting on my own."

Trihn grumbled under her breath, but she didn't see a way out of it. At least it would keep her away from Lydia and Preston's argument.

Ian had no problem in agreeing to come sailing with them. He was competent on the water from years of their families going together. Any earlier tension that had been between them dissipated when she told him what had happened with Lydia, not that they had much time to discuss it before driving with her parents out to the docks.

Plus, she wanted to talk to Renée, who had sent her a bunch of text messages this morning. Apparently, Trihn had drunk-texted her the night before.

What do you mean, you slept with him?

Trihn cringed at that one. Not her finest moment.

Hey. Sorry about the texts last night. I had a little bit to drink.

A little bit? Puh-lease. Tell me what happened!

This morning, I told Lydia about Preston. She didn't believe me at first, but I finally got through to her. She and Preston are arguing right now. I think they're going to break up.

Sounds just like Lydia not to believe you, but at least you got through to her. I always knew he was creepy! But are you going to be okay, T?

Trihn swallowed. *Am I going to be okay?* That was a good question.

Yeah. Don't worry about me.

Someone has to.

About to get to the sailboat. I'll talk to you more about it after!

Yuppie.

Trihn laughed at the comment. Ian raised his eyebrows, and she showed him the text.

"Well, if the shoe fits," he said.

Trihn surveyed his outfit and shrugged in agreement. He was wearing khaki shorts that stopped four inches above his knee, a white polo with a navy-blue sweater hanging from his shoulders, and brown boat shoes. Together, they looked like the definition of *yuppie*, and it hurt her rocker soul.

Once they arrived, they found their boat, and Ian helped her on deck. The sailboat was really more of a yacht, if they were getting technical, and had the option of coming with a captain and small crew that her parents had accepted since Lydia and Preston weren't with them.

The crew easily maneuvered the boat out of the dock and onto open water. She and Ian sat down with her parents to eat lunch out of the picnic basket her mother had prepared earlier this morning. With the absence of Lydia and Preston, there was more food to go around than expected, and they shared with the crew.

Trihn's parents grabbed a bottle of wine and reclined back in chairs at the aft of the ship, leaving Trihn and Ian to enjoy the rest of the afternoon how they saw fit. They found a spot near the front, lay back against the deck, and stared up at the cloudless sky.

"What do you think Lydia and Preston are talking about right now?" Trihn asked. She propped herself on an elbow and looked down at him.

Ian shrugged, meeting her gaze. "How much of an asshole he is?"

She bit her lip. "I hope he's gone by the time we get home."

"Don't we all?" he said.

She dropped back down next to him, and he wrapped his arm around her shoulders. They had done this every summer since they were kids, but suddenly, Lydia's words rang in her mind. Ian liked her. Trihn knew that he cared for her, but she hadn't thought it went further than that. Or maybe she just didn't want it to. She never wanted this to be awkward.

"Thanks for being here for me."

He squeezed her tighter. "You know I'd do anything for you."

"Yeah."

Silence dragged on between them, but it wasn't uncomfortable. It never was.

Trihn was lost in her thoughts about Preston and Lydia. She was stressing over what could be happening, not that she wanted to be there to deal with the fallout, but she just wanted to know what to expect when she got back.

"I really like this," Ian said softly.

"Me, too."

She closed her eyes and let herself drift off. In another world, this could be her life with Ian. Sometimes, she wished that it could be this easy.

But then she knew it couldn't. And wanting something that she couldn't have had only made a mess of her life.

She pulled away from Ian and sat up on the deck.

"Hey," he said, reaching for her hand, "what are you thinking about?"

"Us, I guess."

He raised his eyebrows. "Is there an *us*?"

She met his gaze and shook her head. "I love you, Ian, but you know…you're more like a brother to me."

He nodded, but the pain was on his face.

"I'm sorry."

"I know. I've always known, Trihn. You don't have to apologize. This isn't news to me."

"We've never talked about it before…"

"We never needed to," he said quickly. "I confess that I thought it might be different once I was back in the city again. We'd be closer, spend more time together. It would be easier. We wouldn't have to wait just for vacations."

"Ian," she whispered, "I don't know what to say."

He smiled forlornly. "It was a dream. Nothing more. I knew things weren't going to change."

"You'll find someone better than me at Columbia. I know you will."

"Unlikely. I've known you my whole life, and I haven't found someone like you yet."

Trihn touched his arm in appreciation. It was probably one of the nicest things anyone had ever said to her. She didn't believe it though. Ian had just known her for too long. He would branch out in college and find the perfect woman for him. She knew it.

"And here I am…falling for an asshole."

"Nice guys do finish last."

After a minute, Trihn sheepishly peeked back up at him. "You know, I am sorry."

He shrugged. "Don't be. After all this time, it's good for you to finally know. At least I'll never wonder what could have been."

Trihn decided to let the conversation be. There was so much more she could have said, but she was glad that they had cleared the air. She didn't want him to be hurt over what had happened with Preston, and she definitely didn't want their friendship to suffer because of that—or worse, because of her insensitivity to him.

They spent the remainder of the afternoon lounging on the deck and catching some rays. As their time in the sun came to a close, Trihn realized she was glad that she had come out on the boat even if she was anxious about what she would find when she got home. She had tried not to think too much about it, but as they docked the boat and then drove back to the house, nerves buzzed through her body.

"Let me know if you need me later, okay?" Ian whispered into her ear when they pulled up to the house.

She nodded. She was so tense that she couldn't even speak. She just hurried inside.

None of the lights were on when she walked in, which she took as a good sign. Maybe Preston had already left, and Lydia was napping or something.

She didn't know, but she was ready to find out.

Her feet carried her through the kitchen and then into the dark living room. She flipped the switch on and stumbled backward into the wall. Of all the things she had expected, this was *not* it.

Lydia and Preston were lying on the couch, their clothes were rumpled, and they were making out like it was the last thing they were ever going to do.

"What the fuck?" Trihn cried.

TWENTY-TWO

"I THOUGHT YOU SAID THEY WERE ARGUING, Trihn," Linh said. She had been following close on Trihn's heels and witnessed what was happening on the couch. "I should have realized that was teenager code for wanting to be alone in the house."

Trihn just stared open-mouthed at the display before her. On the inside, she was raging. *What the fuck could have happened in the span of an afternoon to go from Lydia yelling at Preston about cheating on her to making out on the couch?* There was no way they should still be dating. It made zero sense.

"You guys are back!" Lydia said. She quickly straightened and stood. "Already."

"Already," Linh said with a shake of her head. "It's dinnertime, and the Petersons invited us over. You should go...freshen up." Linh raised her eyebrows at the two of them. On a normal day, she wouldn't care what her children were doing and with whom, but she didn't like for it to interfere with her plans.

"Okay, Mom," Lydia said. She brushed her hair over her shoulder and smiled lazily.

"Yes, ma'am," Preston said quickly.

Linh nodded at them, as if her message was clear, and then left for her own room to get ready for dinner.

Trihn just glared at Lydia and Preston. "What the fuck is this?" she demanded as soon as Linh was out of earshot. "When I left, you were screaming at each other, and a few hours later, you're back to making out? What part of 'he was cheating on you,' did you misunderstand, Ly?"

Lydia looked up at Preston, and he nodded.

"Can we go talk?" Lydia asked, nodding toward the empty den.

"We can't talk right here? Are you afraid Mom and Dad will find out what an asshole he is?" Trihn said.

All the anger that she had been feeling this week on vacation was pouring out of her. She wanted to yell and scream at the top of her lungs for everyone to hear. The man who she had loved could not be putting her through this hell right now.

"Trihn, let's just try to be reasonable," Preston said softly, consolingly.

Fuck that.

"Do not try to talk to me like I'm an idiot. I see what is going on here, but I don't understand any of it." She clenched her hands into fists. "Someone, please explain to me how this happened.

What lies did he feed you for you to just ignore the facts?"

"He didn't feed me any lies, Trihn," Lydia said carefully.

"You don't know him if you think that every word he says is the truth. He twists words and the truth, all so that you will believe him…so you'll fall for him."

"Jesus, Trihn," Preston said. "I didn't realize you thought that lowly of me."

"You made me feel this way!" Trihn tried to reel herself in, but it wasn't working. She had never thought that Preston and Lydia would stay together once Lydia had found out the truth. In fact, Trihn had been more worried about hurting her sister. It was apparently all for nothing.

"We actually both wanted to talk to you about this," Lydia said, standing in between Trihn and Preston. "This wasn't how we wanted you to find out that we were staying together."

"What exactly would be a good way for me to find that out?"

"Not like this, obviously."

"Obviously," Trihn repeated. "Just…why?"

"I know that you and Preston were talking for a while this summer," Lydia began.

"Talking," Trihn said tonelessly. *If that's what you call fucking backstage at a ballet and on his dining room table and at the studio and, and, and…*

"Yes, but after Preston and I discussed it, I realized I was only getting half of the story. Just your half. I didn't realize how much more there was to it."

"Oh, this should be a real treat. What exactly *is* Preston's side of the story? And how does what *we* did this summer equate to just talking?" Trihn asked.

"Trihn, I know you told Lydia that I was your boyfriend this summer, but we never defined our relationship like that," Preston said.

She couldn't even meet his gaze. She stared firmly at Lydia. If she looked at Preston, her anger might disintegrate into tears. "I'm not sure the definition is relevant at this point. You and I both know what happened this summer."

"The truth is…Preston and I never defined our relationship this summer either. We never talked about dating exclusively." Lydia shrugged. "I don't normally do that anyway. Until I invited him to come on vacation with us, he hadn't even realized how serious we were and that maybe I would want this to become something more. We both messed around with other people before that point, so that's why he didn't break up with you until right before vacation."

"What?" Trihn asked. Her head snapped to Preston. "We didn't break up. You never broke up with me."

"You've been saying all week that we broke up."

"I said that because you showed up with my sister!" Trihn cried, pointing at Lydia.

"Well, I didn't know that you would be here," Preston admitted. "Lydia invited me on vacation with her, and when the rest of the family showed up, it was a bit of a shock to me. Neither of us wanted to hurt your feelings."

"You're joking right now," Trihn said. Lies, all lies. Everything out of his mouth was one big lie. "Do you ever tell the truth? Did you really work all night that time you didn't answer the phone? Are you fucking that Stephanie girl? That one morning after I stayed the night, was it really someone else who was calling rather than work? How about we just check your cell phone right now and see if all the lies are unraveled?"

"Trihn!" Lydia cried. "I'm sorry about all the stuff that happened during this vacation, but you don't need to go accusing Preston of being a liar. You told me what happened. He told me what happened. I can't preach free love and then be pissed when I'm not even in a serious relationship." She intertwined her fingers with Preston's and leaned into his arm. "I'm ready for this to be serious now."

Trihn's eyes popped out of her head. "You're seriously choosing *him* over me?"

"It's not a choice, Trihn," Lydia said. "I choose both of you. We can make this work."

"That's where you're wrong. You're so very wrong, Lydia. I can't make this work." Trihn shook her head in disbelief. "We're about to move in together, and you're dating...*him*. I won't live there if you're with him."

"Trihn, don't make this an ultimatum."

"It became one the minute you cared more about him than me," Trihn said. She shook her head and backed up a few steps. "And you chose him."

"This is a choice you're making. You're choosing to walk out."

"You're right," Trihn said. "I am. Fuck this."

Then, she turned and ran from the house. She ran from the bullshit that she considered her life and the torment of seeing Preston with her sister and the utter inhumanity of her own flesh and blood choosing a boy over her.

TWENTY-THREE

TRIHN'S FEET CARRIED HER TO THE PETERSONS'. She found Ian in his room on his computer. Before she could get a word out, she broke down into sobs.

"What? What happened?" He reached for her and pulled her onto his lap. "Trihn, are you all right? Tell me what happened!"

"She…chose…him…over me," Trihn said between hiccuping tears.

She wrapped her arms around his neck and let her tears stain his polo. Words were failing her as her heart shattered into as many pieces as there were stars in the night sky.

"She did what?"

Trihn sniffed a few times before the tears subsided enough for her to have a coherent conversation. "They talked it out when we were gone, and she believed all his lies. He told her that he wasn't serious with her until she invited him on vacation, and then he broke up with me, which wasn't what happened. I just said that he broke up with me because I saw him with her. When I tried to explain, she wouldn't even listen to me. Then, I told her that I couldn't be around her if she was dating him, and she chose *him*."

"I just…can't believe Lydia would do this. You're her sister."

"Yeah, well, that doesn't seem to matter to her," Trihn said. She wiped at her eyes. "Will you do something for me, Ian?"

"You know I will, but why do I feel like I'm not going to like this?" he asked. His hand was gently rubbing her back, trying to soothe her. Yet she couldn't be soothed, not after what had happened.

"Take me into the city?"

"This again?" he asked. "Maybe you should sleep on this. Try to talk to Lydia again in the morning."

"And what? Wait for her to get firmly planted in her beliefs? Lydia is staunch in her opinions."

"Like someone else I know."

Her gaze was as hard as steel, and she shot out of his lap. "She won't believe me! I'm not going to pretend any longer to be okay with what's going on. Are you going to help me or not?"

He nodded his head. "Of course, I'll help you."

Trihn hurried back to her house, purposely going in through the rear door to avoid her family. She did *not* want to have a run-in with anyone after the catastrophe of a conversation with Lydia and Preston. She listened intently at the stairway until she knew the coast was clear. Then, she dashed up the stairs and entered her room. It was exactly how she had left it this morning before she had run to Ian's after hearing Lydia and Preston having sex.

With a huff, Trihn threw a bunch of clothes along with her headphones into a backpack. Then, she snatched up her purse and traded out her sandals for her sneakers. The rest would just have to stay. She threw the backpack over her shoulder and then inched out of her room.

Lydia's door was closed, and Trihn could hear her shuffling around inside. There was no chance of Trihn seeing her at least. She darted down the stairs and to the door. She had almost made it outside when she heard someone behind her.

"I have a feeling your mother isn't going to like this," Gabriel said, stopping her in her tracks.

She dropped her hand and turned to face her dad. He was seated on the darkened deck with an iPad in his hand.

"Hey, Dad," she said softly.

He sighed, put the iPad on the side table next to him, and stood. "Want to tell me what's going on with you and Lydia?"

Trihn bit her lip. "Nothing is going on."

"You have a backpack hanging off your shoulder and tennis shoes on your feet, and you're sneaking out the back door. You always act like this when you and Lydia fight, ever since you were this high," he said, holding his hand up to his knee. "Now, you don't have to tell me the problem, but you do have to be held accountable for the fact that it looks like you're running away."

Trihn dropped her bag. *Busted.* There was no way she was going to get away now. "I don't know what to tell you."

"I really don't want to get your mother involved. Work has been extra stressful lately, and she needs this time to relax." Gabriel walked over to Trihn and picked up the pack. "Is this something that you can resolve with Lydia without your mother knowing anything was wrong?"

She shook her head. "No way."

He sighed. "I had a feeling you would say that. Am I right in assuming Ian is involved in the escape route?"

"Well, I'm not leaving now."

Her dad smiled. "I know this is hard to believe, but I've known you your whole life."

Trihn snorted.

"It has to be serious for you to resort to drastic measures. The last time this happened, you were in the fifth grade and Lydia punched you in the face the day before picture day. You ran away, and we couldn't find you for three hours."

Trihn laughed at the memory. "I completely forgot about that."

"I'm still not sure why she hit you, but you got over it after you had your space." He pulled a set of car keys out of his pocket and offered them to Trihn.

"What…"

"I saw you come in earlier. I think I know my kids." He dropped them in her open hand. "Make Ian drive."

Her jaw hit the floor. "Thank you so much," she said, throwing her arms around her dad. "You're the best."

"Just be safe, and don't worry about your mother. I'll take care of it."

"I love you, Dad."

"I love you too. Just promise to try to make up with your sister once you start to feel better."

Trihn nodded. "I will."

If I ever feel better...

She shouldered her backpack again and texted Ian to tell him to meet her in her garage.

He showed up a couple of minutes later. "Trihn?" he called softly. "What are we doing in here?"

"Over here," she said. "Dad caught me."

"Shit!"

She tossed him the keys, and he snatched them out of the air with his left hand.

He looked at her in confusion. "What are these for?"

"Dad said you should drive."

"He's letting you go?" he asked in disbelief.

"Yep. Said he had seen this coming all along and then handed me the keys. Said he would handle Mom and everything."

"Whoa! That was unexpected. I was going to try to sneak the keys to the Beamer and suffer my father's wrath, but this is way better."

Trihn laughed. "Way better."

They jumped into her parents' silver Mercedes SUV, and Ian maneuvered it out of the garage. Trihn rolled down the window and let the evening air whip her hair around her face. She plugged her iPhone into the system. Ian looked over at her with worry in his eyes. They didn't see eye to eye on music. While she could appreciate almost anything and she could dance to even more than that, her heart belonged to rock music.

Fall Out Boy blasted through the speakers, and Ian just shook his head. "I knew this was coming."

"That's what she said," Trihn said.

She relaxed back in the passenger seat and let the tunes relax her. Driving away from everyone and everything might not be the most mature choice, but being miles, rather than feet, away from Preston was good for her psyche. She was already feeling more like herself.

But after three hours of on and off traffic, even the music couldn't chill her nerves or her desire to be out of the car. She pulled her mane of hair back into a ponytail and tapped her foot. She could see the skyline from the distance, which only made her more anxious to be there.

"Just remind me of the turn for your place. It's been a while since I've been there," Ian told her.

Trihn shot up in her seat. "Wait."

"What?" he asked, his eyes widening with concern.

"Take me into Manhattan."

Ian deflated. "Why? It's late. I'm tired. I've ignored about a hundred phone calls from my mom. I just want to get somewhere and relax before being demolished tomorrow."

"I know for a fact that your parents are not going to demolish you. Anyway, I think my dad will smooth the whole thing over," she told him. "But still…into Manhattan we go."

"Seriously?"

"Seriously."

"Do you have a reason?"

"I need to do something," she said conspiratorially.

"Is that supposed to reassure me?"

"Probably not."

Ian shook his head. He had just driven her three hours back into the city on a whim, so he wasn't exactly going to question her next move even if he probably should.

"We'll have to find parking somewhere close. It's probably going to be a fortune." She groaned, directing him down another side street through the maze. "There!"

He pulled up beside another car and then expertly parallel parked the SUV.

"Whoa. For a kid from the suburbs, you're good at that."

"I actually passed my driver's test, Trihn."

"Yeah, well, I passed."

"The third time," he mumbled.

"Who needs to drive in New York City?" she demanded, stepping out of the car.

Ian just laughed at her and followed her down the street. "Where are we headed anyway?"

She rounded the corner and stopped in front of the familiar building. Her heart wrenched as she remembered the last time she had been here— Preston's insistence before they had gotten to the show, the way he'd looked at her when she brought him to her underground world, the waves of desire when he'd watched her dance, the hungry glint in his eye and the casual way he'd offered her a threesome, as if it were her idea to begin with. She should have seen the signs. But she didn't and hadn't wanted to.

"Where is here?" Ian asked. He cast his gaze around the dark, stopping at the seemingly empty location.

"Slipper."

TWENTY-FOUR

"WHAT IS SLIPPER?" IAN ASKED CAUTIOUSLY.

"It's an underground prostitution ring I've been a part of for the past couple of years," she deadpanned.

She watched Ian's face go from horror to confusion to embarrassment.

Then, she started laughing. "I can't see right now, but how red are your cheeks?"

"You're not really a part of an…"

"Underground prostitution ring," she filled in for him.

"Yeah."

"No, I'm not. It's a burlesque club. They dance and have acrobatic routines at night."

"Okay," he said skeptically. "Why are we here?"

"Because I dance here."

"Here? At a burlesque club."

She nodded.

"I never knew you did that kind of thing," he said. "I thought it was all ballet."

"Well, I never told anyone."

Here was something she had painstakingly tried to hide from the outside world. She'd tried to keep this hidden in an attempt to be the right person at the right time.

She compartmentalized parts of herself for the various people that she was around. With Renée, she was the strict ballerina with her rocker edge. With Ian, she was the yuppie heiress to a fashion legacy. With Lydia, she was the baby who idolized her older sister. With Francesca, she was a fun-loving model party girl who was into high fashion. With Cassidy, she was the lithe pole dancer willing to try almost anything. With Preston…she had thought she had allowed him to see all the parts of her, but that didn't mean that he'd fit the pieces together. It just meant that he had seen the puzzle and scattered the pieces.

Maybe if she started here, she could knit those fragments back together and try to be all of herself at once. In time, she wouldn't have to hide the different sides of her personality. She could just be Trihn.

"You can stay out here if you want," she told Ian before marching down the steps.

The woman at the front door clapped her hands together when she saw Trihn approaching. "Oh my God, are you performing tonight, lovey dove?" She was dressed even more radical tonight in a lingerie corset set and high heels. Her bob had been replaced by a crazy wig with long flowing gray curls.

"No, not tonight. I just need to talk to Cassidy. Is she performing tonight?"

"She's back there, but I don't know how much talking you'll get done. Chick is a little emotional."

"What do you mean?" Trihn scrunched her eyebrows together.

"Haven't you heard?"

"Heard what?"

"Oh, dear," she said, putting her hand to her chest. "I'll have to let her break the news to you."

Trihn frowned. "Is it serious? Is she okay?"

"I'll let you in at the end of this set, and you can go talk to her." The girl's eyes moved high above Trihn, and she smiled devilishly. "And who do we have here?"

Trihn whipped around and saw Ian coming down the steps. "What are you doing?"

"Not leaving you alone in a place like this," Ian said. He hurried to her side.

Trihn laughed. "No need to protect me. I'm probably going to need to protect you."

The applause rang out through the rusty black door, and the woman jumped. "Time for you two to head on inside. Good seeing you again, Trihn."

She nodded at the girl and then dragged Ian inside Slipper before he could protest. His eyes were as big as saucers as he took in the giant room that looked like a real court amid a fairy tale. It was brilliant, and she always marveled at it every time she was inside. But she knew for a fact that Ian had never seen anything like it.

"Come on. We're going backstage." She took his arm and pulled him through the room and to a side curtain.

Someone recognized her and pointed in the direction of where they had last seen Cassidy.

They stopped in front of the women's changing room, and she left Ian at the door. "This won't take long."

He nervously eyed his surroundings. "Please don't."

She laughed and then went in through the door. It was easy to find Cassidy. She stood out even in a crowded room. Besides her bright red pixie cut, there was just something about her.

As if feeling eyes on her, Cassidy whipped around. She was in a studded red outfit to match her hair and spiked black boots. She normally performed barefoot, but Trihn had seen her in the boots, too, and it was insane.

"Trihn!" Cassidy barreled through the other performers to get to Trihn's side. "Come to dance tonight?"

"Not tonight," Trihn said. She took a deep breath. She could do this. "For good. I'm in. I accept the offer."

Cassidy's face fell. "Oh, Trihn…"

"What?"

Trihn hadn't really thought this through when she realized they were near the city. She had just decided that she wasn't going to be afraid to show the real her anymore. She enjoyed dancing and performing. She loved the thrill of it, and maybe her family would hate it, but they would get over it.

"I'm so glad that you decided to accept the position, but I was actually offered an opportunity that I just couldn't refuse."

"What kind of opportunity?" Trihn asked.

A smile spread across Cassidy's beautiful face. "Dancing in Las Vegas! As a main event at a new

Cirque show they're opening up next year. I never thought I'd be selected for something like that. I got the call just this morning, and I was going to call you this weekend after I told the Slipper crew."

Trihn's mouthed dropped open. "Oh my God, that's amazing, Cass! It's a dream come true. I know you've been auditioning for that kind of thing but haven't heard back."

"I never thought it would happen in a million years!"

"You should have. You're brilliant," Trihn said, seeing her plan disintegrate.

"Look, this is going to sound crazy, but hear me out." Cassidy said. She grabbed Trihn's hands. "Come with me!"

Trihn laughed. "What?"

"Come with me to Vegas! I'll have my own place. You can get a job dancing or teaching even! Didn't you say they have a fashion school out there, too? You could go to school while we dance! Think about how awesome it would be!" Cassidy said enthusiastically.

"I don't know," Trihn said reluctantly. "I'm supposed to attend NYU in a few weeks."

"NYU will always be there! How often will you be young and wild and free to do whatever you want in your life? Just this once!" Cassidy said. "I know it's crazy to just up and leave your life. I can't believe I'm doing it, but at the same time…I can't wait."

"Cass, it was a stretch for me to take this dancing job in the city. I can't imagine moving across the country to do it. Everyone that I know is here in New York."

"Well, that won't be true in a couple of days." Cassidy reminded her, "I'll be gone."

Trihn shook her head. "I don't know. I mean...wow! Thank you for inviting me. I just...I have never, ever thought about leaving here."

"That's why it's the time to do it. Everyone dreams their whole lives about living in New York City for just a short while, but we grew up here. Let's go somewhere else, and if we're meant to come back to the city, we will." Cassidy winked at her. "NYC Dance House created beautiful dancers out of us. It would be a shame to waste that talent so young!"

"Renée is still dancing," Trihn admitted.

"See?" Cassidy grabbed Trihn's hand and twirled her in a circle. "Sin City awaits the dancing duo!"

"I...I'll have to think about it. I have a lot going on right now."

"That creep you were with?" Cassidy asked, arching an eyebrow.

"You thought he was a creep?" Trihn asked in surprise.

"Uh...yeah. He had slimeball written all over him. I would have warned you, but you were in way over your head."

"Yeah, I guess I was," she said softly.

"Cassidy!" the stage manager called. "You're up on deck, honey."

"That's my cue, love. Think about it. Either way, I'll be in Vegas by Saturday, and if you don't come with, I'm going to miss you."

Cassidy pulled her into a fierce hug, and then they walked out together. Cassidy rushed over to stand by the stage entrance, and Trihn found Ian standing amid a cloud of women. She laughed, but her head was elsewhere.

What would it be like to take Cassidy's advice? Could I leave everything I'd ever known behind to go to Las Vegas on a whim?

Sure, she had applied to Las Vegas State's Teena Hart School of Design as a backup. Her mother had discovered Teena Hart out of the LV State fashion school before it had been anything. Her designs now were on runways around the world, and she had spent a small fortune building the school into something that competed with the top-tier fashion programs. It still wasn't NYU or Parsons, but it wasn't looked down upon either.

What the hell am I thinking? I couldn't leave my entire life behind to run away to Vegas.

Could I?

TWENTY-FIVE

TRIHN COULDN'T STOP THINKING ABOUT IT.

Ever since Cassidy had asked her to go to Las Vegas, it was like a virus infecting her brain. She silently weighed the pros and cons of what that could mean for her life and also wondered if it would even be possible for her to start at LV State on such short notice. The fact that she was thinking about it at all worried her.

Her father had sent her back home, so she could cool off about what was going on with Lydia. But the longer Trihn was here, the more she saw Preston on every corner. It didn't matter how many times she had been in the city before him. Somehow, the summer had reshaped her worldview on her own hometown. He was everywhere. And worse yet, he would be everywhere with Lydia in the fall.

Trihn's stomach couldn't handle it. Maybe if Lydia and Preston were separated, then she could stay in New York and begin to fix her relationship with Lydia. She could change the way she saw every corner and diner and coffee shop that she associated with Preston. They could be sisters having fun at the same college. It could be fine.

But Lydia had chosen to stay with Preston, and they weren't fine.

And it was worse than that. She had always looked up to Lydia. Trihn had wanted to be her so badly when she was younger. They had gone to the same private school. They had danced at the same dance studio. It only made sense for them to move in together and go to college together. They shared everything—even a boyfriend.

If I move in with Lydia and go to NYU, would I grow to be the better person I want to be?

"Are you okay?" Ian asked.

Trihn had almost forgotten that he was driving as they went to the NYC Dance House to pick up Renée and fill her in on what had happened.

"Maybe. Cassidy just gave me a lot to think about."

"Well, I'm trying not to think about all the offers I got while in that place." His blush reached his ears. "And you wanted to dance there?"

She nodded. "I did."

"I never would have guessed."

"You've known me my whole life, and I'm still full of surprises."

"I like you that way," he said with a smile.

"Yeah," she whispered, leaning against the door and looking out at her city as it sped by.

Renée was waiting for them on the front steps of the Dance House when they drove up. Her black hair was tied up into a sleek bun, and she had on a pink skirt over her tights and leotard.

"I see how it is," Trihn said as Renée climbed into the SUV. "Can't even bother to get decent for us."

Renée threw her dance bag into the back and plopped down. "I don't want to hear it from you, missy. You ran away from home."

"Technically, I ran *to* home," Trihn corrected her.

"Well, fill me in on the details, and let's get something to eat. I'm starving. I need a burger."

"So, you're not on the Juilliard diet yet?"

Renée grabbed a pointe shoe from her bag and threw it at the back of Trihn's head. Trihn dodged it and laughed.

"Oh, hey, Ian," Renée said. "Long time no see."

"Good to see you again. Congratulations on Juilliard," Ian said, veering them out of Manhattan and back toward Trihn's home in Brooklyn.

"And you'll be at…Columbia?" she asked.

"Yeah, that's right. We'll both be on the Upper West Side."

"That's still terrifying to me. Moving from the Bronx to the Upper anything," she admitted. Renée shuddered. "All right. Give me the deets."

So, Trihn filled her in on everything that she had missed while Trihn was on vacation. All the sordid details of the past week spilled out of her in a long, detailed diatribe. It sounded pretty awful and pathetic when it was all displayed in that fashion. She kind of hated herself for allowing something like this to happen, but mostly, she despised Preston for the kind of person he turned women into. She and Lydia were supposed to be strong, independent women, and they were both acting like idiots over a man.

They reached Trihn's place by the end of the conversation, and they all bustled inside. Trihn started whipping up sandwiches for them since most of the good places nearby were closed. She could have ordered in, but it was somehow calming to have something to do while she finished her story.

"So, I went to see Cassidy," Trihn told Renée and Ian.

He was still listening to the story he already knew, but this next part would be new to him.

"Cassidy Kincaid?" Renée asked, her eyes wide. "You still hang out with her?"

Trihn nodded. "I've been dancing with her after the studio closes for about two years now."

"Why didn't you say anything?"

"No one else really got along with her. She didn't fit the ballerina mold," Trihn explained. "And she's not dancing ballet anymore. She's been working in a burlesque club and pole dancing."

"Wow. Good for her," Renée said.

"Wait, really?"

"Yeah. I mean, she was a great ballerina, but I could see her being amazing at anything. Plus, I bet she's happier in that atmosphere, doing what she loves."

"She is," Trihn agreed. "She offered me a job pole dancing, but then she was offered a job for a Cirque show in Las Vegas."

"Holy shit! That's fantastic!"

"Wow," Ian said. Even he was impressed.

"Yeah." Trihn looked down at her hands. "She asked me to go with her."

Both of her best friends were silent. She peeked up at them, and they both looked stunned.

"But you start school in a few weeks," Ian reasoned.

"And what would you do there? What about fashion design?" Renée asked.

"I know. I know. I told her I'd think about it."

"Are you thinking about it?" Renée asked at the same time as Ian said, "Seriously?"

"I don't know." She sighed. "I'm tired of living in Lydia's shadow, and I can't live with her if she's with Preston. I told her that, but I don't think she believes me. I can't do it."

"That doesn't mean you walk away from everything!" Ian said.

"Shh," Renée chided him. "This isn't our decision. You're serious, aren't you?"

Trihn nodded. "I think I am. I mean, at least I'm seriously considering it. Renée, you're going to Juilliard to pursue your dreams, and, Ian, you're going to Columbia to pursue yours."

"Aren't you going to NYU to pursue yours?" Ian asked. "Fashion design?"

"Yeah. I want to design fashion, but I also don't want to give up everything else in my life to do it. It's not wrong to want to pursue all your dreams, is it?" Trihn asked.

She didn't want to stop dancing, and maybe one day, she would even want to model again. She felt so limited, quitting everything else to pursue just one thing. That wasn't what college was supposed to be about. It was supposed to broaden her horizons, not limit them.

"It sounds crazy," Ian said.

Renée shrugged. "A little crazy, but if you think it's right, then do it."

"I don't know. I don't know what feels right," Trihn told them.

"Take this time while you're here, without your family telling you what to do, and you'll figure it out." Renée covered Trihn's hand with her own. "Do what's best for you. If that means staying in New York and going to NYU but getting a dorm with a stranger and not living with Lydia, then do that. If it means making amends with Lydia and starting fresh, that's fine, too. If it means taking this opportunity to go to Las Vegas…well, that's up to you, too. You have to think about you. It's the only way you'll be happy."

Trihn took the next two days to think over Cassidy's offer. She didn't want to just jump into something crazy, but she did want to actually consider it.

On the day that her family was supposed to come back to the city, she had made up her mind. She dialed Cassidy's number and waited.

"Hello?" Cassidy answered.

"Cassidy?" Trihn said.

"Hey, Trihn! You caught me at a good time. I was just packing a bunch of stuff for Las Vegas and sending it with the movers."

"That's really awesome."

"Why does it sound like this is the last time I'm going to hear from you?" Cassidy asked.

Trihn took a deep breath. "I've made up my mind about your offer, and I just wanted to call and talk to you about it."

"Well, will you at least promise to come visit?" Cassidy asked. "It's supposed to be so much fun there."

Trihn's stomach flipped as she broke the news to her friend, "I'm in."

TWENTY-SIX

EXPLAINING TO HER FATHER over the phone that she'd be moving to Las Vegas the day they came back from vacation was easier than she'd thought it would be.

"I understand," he said into the phone. "I thought the distance would make you decide that you wanted to make up with your sister, but it seems that's not the case."

"No. I think I'm ready for something new, somewhere else. I want to be my own person."

"And not follow behind Lydia?" he asked.

"Exactly. And this isn't all about Lydia either. I was offered something amazing. I'm only young once, and I want to embrace it."

"I always knew my wild child was still in there," he said with a laugh.

She ended the call with tears in her eyes as she packed a suitcase. She was supposed to meet Cassidy at the airport in a couple of hours. She was only bringing enough stuff to get her through the first week or two before classes started. Her dad had agreed to send the rest to her once they had things sorted out with the university, and she had her own place.

She still couldn't believe that she was going to move across the country, but at the same time, she was so excited.

Trihn called for a cab to take her to LaGuardia Airport. With her luggage, a cab would be way easier than dealing with the subway.

Nearly an hour later, the cab driver was unloading her bags in front of the terminal. She paid him and watched him drive away.

This was real. It was really happening.

She wheeled her luggage inside and printed off her boarding pass. Her phone chimed.

Already through security! Easy, peasy.

Trihn laughed at the message from Cassidy.

A knot formed in her throat, and she tried to hold back the tears. No matter how right the decision felt, she was still leaving her home behind and without even a proper good-bye.

As she walked toward security, she said her own farewell to her family. She knew they would visit, and she would be back for the holidays, but it wouldn't be the same.

"Trihn!"

Trihn whipped around in confusion as her name was yelled from across the terminal. *What the hell?*

And there was Lydia, dashing across the room like a madwoman. She stopped in front of Trihn and rested her hands on her knees, breathing heavily.

"What are you doing here, Lydia?" Trihn asked, crossing her arms over her chest.

"Dad...told us...in the car," Lydia said.

"And what? You made him drive you here, hoping to catch me?"

"Yes."

"Okay. What are you doing here?"

"You can't leave! Las Vegas, Trihn? What the hell is that?" Lydia asked, catching her breath.

"I can leave. In fact, I already have my ticket and my bags packed, and I'm leaving now."

"You can't do this because of me," Lydia said.

"Why is everything always about you, Lydia? I'm doing this for me. I'm doing this because I was given a great opportunity, and I can study fashion anywhere. I don't need to be here in the city."

"But we were supposed to live together."

"You made your choice about that," Trihn said. "I'm making my choice. This is my choice."

"You're overreacting about this whole thing, and you're going to regret it."

"No," Trihn said, "you will."

"He didn't even love you," Lydia said harshly.

Trihn cringed. No, she knew that. He hadn't loved her. That was fine. She could move on...eventually. "Well, he doesn't love you either."

"Yes, he does," Lydia said. Her voice was indignant.

"Did he tell you that we slept together?" Trihn finally admitted.

215

She hated bringing it up, but Lydia had to know. She had to know everything even if it was utterly humiliating to Trihn.

"Well, I figured as much."

"At the beach house," Trihn clarified.

"What?" Lydia asked in surprise.

"Yep. Your precious boyfriend, the one who claims to love you, slept with me when he knew that we were related and after he knew you two were 'serious,'" Trihn said, putting air quotes around the last word. "He doesn't love you. He's just using you like he uses everyone else."

"You slept with him in the Hamptons?"

Trihn paled and nodded. To her greatest regret and shame, she'd done it..

"So…it wasn't just him. My own sister was in on it." Lydia's hands shook. "When?"

"Lydia—"

"When?" she demanded.

"The night of the Petersons' party."

Lydia covered her mouth. "We had sex the next morning."

"I know." She swallowed hard. "I heard it."

"Where?"

"Why are we doing this?" Trihn asked. "You don't need all the details. It happened. It was a mistake. I'm sorry that we did it, but you have to know now that Preston is a dirty scumbag. He's not right for you. He's not right for anyone!"

"Where?" Lydia repeated crossly.

Trihn sighed and huffed, "On the pool deck."

"How could you do this to me?" Lydia asked. Tears welled in her eyes, and she looked like someone had kicked her puppy.

"I didn't mean to do anything to you, Lydia. It's Preston. He's the manipulator. Can't you see that?" Trihn reached for Lydia's hands and held them tight together.

Lydia wrenched out of her grasp. "I see all right. I see fine now. You want him for yourself. That's what this whole thing is about."

"What?" Trihn asked, dumbfounded. "I do *not* want to be with Preston."

"You think he's the manipulator and he's the bad person, but he's not the only one, Trihn. You are too. You don't care about me," she said, taking a step away from her sister.

"I do care! Of course I care!" Trihn said.

"If you cared, then why didn't you tell me when you first knew I was dating Preston? Why did you wait several days? How could you fuck him behind my back? I was at the party, *waiting* for him to return, and you had sex with him." Lydia looked at her like she didn't even know her own sister.

Trihn couldn't explain. "I loved him," she whispered.

But it was the wrong thing to say.

"Of course you did," Lydia said sarcastically. "That's the reason you slept with him that night…because you loved him. Are you sure it wasn't because you wanted something that was mine, just like you always have?"

Trihn's mouth dropped open. "I didn't."

"Save it for someone who will believe you." Lydia wiped a tear from her eye. "You know I was coming here to tell you to come home. I was going to tell you that if it meant that much to you…I wouldn't work things out with Preston. I like him—a lot," she said, her eyes going wide, "a lot more than anyone else I've dated. Maybe I love him. But I would have ended it because I love my sister that much. Now...I think maybe you should get on that plane."

"Lydia, you can't be serious."

"I am serious."

Trihn stared at her sister in shock. "I made a mistake. I slept with a guy who I thought I loved and who I'd dated seriously all summer. My first real boyfriend. I was—I am heartbroken. I went to tell you what happened, Lydia, and your response went from breakup to make up in a few short hours. You didn't *care* about my feelings. You don't care about how I'm feeling right now."

Trihn crossed her arms over her chest and glanced away from her sister. "And then you chose him over me without hesitating. So, maybe you're right. Maybe I should get on that plane. Because I know what is waiting for me if I stay," she said, turning to boldly stare at her sister, "and it's not so welcoming."

"I told you that I didn't think it had to be a choice. You're the one who chose," Lydia said.

"Yeah, right. Keep telling yourself that. What did you expect me to do? After what happened at the beach house, there was no going back, not with the kind of person Preston is. I mean, what kind of guy leaves his girlfriend who is perfectly willing to have sex with him to seek out her drunk sister in the middle of the night?" Trihn raised her eyebrows in question.

When Lydia didn't have an immediate answer, Trihn nodded her head. "That's what I thought." She picked up her suitcase off the ground where she had left it and headed for security.

"So, you're just going to leave?" Lydia cried.

Trihn turned back to her sister and shrugged. "You left first."

As she walked into the line and handed her boarding pass to the person at security, a sad smile hit her face. She knew she was moving in the right direction even if she felt like she was in a free fall. Her plans were uncertain. Her potential career choices might be going up in flames. Her life was a total mess.

But she couldn't be happy here.

"Final destination, Las Vegas." The woman smiled at her. "Business or pleasure?"

Trihn smiled back. "Both."

The End

ACKNOWLEDGMENTS

THANK YOU to each and every one of you who helped me write this novel. It was hands-down one of the hardest things I'd ever written because I was so busy getting married and moving. So, thank you to the people who put in the hours to ensure I got through this book and helped every step of the way: Jessica Carnes, Rebecca Kimmerling, Diana Peterfreund, Lori Francis, Polly Matthews, Christy Peckham, Katie Miller, Lauren Blakely, all the girls of FYW, Jovana Shirley of Unforeseen Editing, Sarah Hansen of Okay Creations, Jenn Sterling, and many, many more!

ABOUT THE AUTHOR

K.A. LINDE is the *USA Today* bestselling author of the Avoiding series and the All That Glitters series as well as seven additional novels.

She grew up as a military brat traveling the United States and even landing for a brief stint in Australia.

She has a master's degree in political science from the University of Georgia and is the current head coach of the Duke University dance team.

k.a. linde

An avid traveler, reader, and bargain hunter, K.A. currently lives in Chapel Hill, North Carolina, with her husband and two super adorable puppies.

K.A. Linde loves to hear from her readers!

You can contact her at kalinde45@gmail.com or visit her online at one of the following sites:

www.kalinde.com

www.facebook.com/authorkalinde

@authorkalinde

Turn the Page to Reveal the First Chapter of the Conclusion to Trihn's Story in:

PLATINUM

RELEASING SPRING 2016!

Read the Other Books in the All That Glitters Series Here:

BRYNA'S STORY

Diamonds (#1)
Gold (#2)

TRIHN'S STORY

Platinum (#3)

STACIA'S STORY

Silver (#4)

PLATINUM

THIS WAS A VERY BAD IDEA.

Trihn's sighed heavily as she stared at the name on the screen of her phone and avoided the knowing looks from her best friends, Bryna and Stacia.

"Just don't invite him," Bryna said irritably.

"I'm not inviting him," Trihn snapped back.

Trihnity Hamilton had been dating her boyfriend, Neal, for over a year and a half. They had met and fell for each other over their mutual love for artistic endeavors. He was a graphic design major while she studied fashion design with a focus in art. Unfortunately, that lifestyle didn't exactly fit with Trihn's love for partying.

Or so Neal said.

Frankly, Bryna flat out hated him, and at this point Stacia barely tolerated him. The disconnect between the two most important things in her life, her friends and her boyfriend, was causing some…unnecessary strain.

"I'm just going to answer this and then we can go," Trihn said. She turned away from her friends before anyone could say anything to change her mind. And she knew Bryna would try.

"I just don't think it's a good idea," Trihn heard Bryna say to Stacia behind her back.

"Leave it be, Bri," Stacia said.

Trihn took a breath and answered the phone with forced enthusiasm. "Hey!"

"Hey, what are you up to tonight?" Neal asked.

Trihn twirled her long brown-to-blonde ombre around her finger and tried to calm herself down. She was *not* going to argue with Neal tonight. Not about going to the club for a girl's night. He'd understand.

He would.

She would just keep telling herself that.

Her stomach knotted anyway. Twisting and turning against her will as fear crept up her spine. No matter how much she tried to tamp it down, it just slithered its way back up.

She took a deep breath. "I was just about to head out with Bri and Stacia. We're going to this club that's having some kind of crazy dance party…"

"Let me guess," he said dryly. "Bryna's suggestion?"

"Maya actually!" she said, trying to keep pep in her voice. "She's meeting us there later after she gets off work."

Maya was their favorite bartender at the local bar they frequented, Posse. It was located just off the Las Vegas State campus where Trihn was starting the second semester of her sophomore year.

"I see. Well, never mind then."

"I would *totally* invite you," Trihn insisted. Bryna coughed noisily behind her. Trihn swiveled around and glared at her and Stacia. "But…it's a girl's night. I'm so sorry. I didn't know you were getting back early. I should have checked with your schedule."

Stacia snorted and shook her head. Bryna looked like she was ready to rip the phone out of her hand and tell Neal exactly what he could do with his schedule.

"It's fine, Trihn. I was just going to see if I could come over since I just got back from San Francisco."

"I know," she whispered.

Over winter break, Neal had had an internship for graphic design in San Francisco, where his parents lived. It was a continuation of his work from last summer. She had only seen him for a couple days when her parents had flown him out to New York City for New Year's.

He had gotten back to Las Vegas two days early. She had thought he wouldn't be in town until the Sunday before school started, but his parents had decided otherwise. She felt bad that she already had plans and would have run over there in a heartbeat, but Maya never got out of work to hang out with them. She couldn't pass up the opportunity. She figured she would just see Neal tomorrow and all would be fine.

"So," she said softly.

The silence stretched between them as she waited for him to say something. She bit her lip and fought against the growing awkwardness in their relationship. When he had visited her only a couple weeks ago, things had been strange. He'd been more interested in getting to know her sister, Lydia, than spending time with Trihn. She and Lydia still had a strained relationship after what had happened post high school graduation, and it didn't help that Trihn had *another* boyfriend who seemed enamored by Lydia.

"I'll just talk to you later or something," Neal said after a few silent minutes. "I'll probably go to The Kiln since you don't want to see me."

Trihn cringed. She actually hated The Kiln. It was an artistic dream in theory. A bar with live music and slam poetry under the same roof as a pottery studio. But in reality everyone sat around and bemoaned the state of the art movement or lack there of in America, got high as fuck, and then made art with their bodies...with whoever was around. It wasn't uncommon for the place to turn into an orgy.

"It's not that I don't want to see you," she insisted. "I do really want to see you, but we've had this planned for awhile..."

"Okay."

"But...do you have to go to The Kiln?" she managed to get out. He *knew* she hated that place. It was a breeding ground for bad behavior. All the while, he claimed that the clubs she went to were bad.

"You're going out to some club to get wasted with your friends and basically have sex on the dance floor, and you're asking *me* to not go out?" he asked in a tone that brokered no argument.

"I'm not going to have *sex* on the dance floor," she argued anyway. "But I know that people do at Kiln. It's just…gross."

"Trihn, don't lecture me about what I can and can't do."

"I wasn't," she whimpered. "I just…"

"Look, I'm going to go. If you decide to stop fucking around and want to take us seriously, then come to Kiln and we can talk."

"I…"

The line went dead in her hand, and she nearly screamed. How dare he insinuate that she was going out to fuck around, and she didn't take their relationship seriously!

She was the one putting all the effort into their relationship. Half the time he was pissed off about what she was doing and who she was hanging out with. It was blatantly clear he didn't trust her. She didn't get it, because she had never done anything to make him think otherwise. She was as loyal as they came.

After the fiasco with Preston, she couldn't even imagine fooling around behind someone's back. It pissed her off all over again.

She tried to rein in her emotions. The last thing she wanted was to be in a bad mood when she went out with the girls. Things with Neal would work out. They always did. He would get mad and lash out, but when they got back together, everything would be fine. He was just frustrated.

"All right," she said, dropping the phone to her side. "Are you guys ready to party?"

Bryna and Stacia exchanged equally sympathetic looks. They knew things between she and Neal were rocky even if they had only heard half of the conversation.

"Is everything okay?" Stacia asked hesitantly.

"I really don't want to talk about it," Trihn said stiffly. "Let's just go have a good time."

She hoped that was still possible.

CPSIA information can be obtained at www.ICGtesting.com
Printed in the USA
BVOW06s1126030116

431650BV00024B/335/P